WITHDRAWN
NDSU

A CURE OF SOULS

BY
MAY SINCLAIR

THE BELFRY
THE TREE OF HAVEN
MARY OLIVIER
THE COMBINED MAZE
A DEFENCE OF IDEALISM
JOURNAL OF IMPRESSIONS IN BELGIUM
LIFE AND DEATH OF HARRIETT FREAN
THE ROMANTIC
ANNE SEVERN AND THE FIELDINGS
THE NEW IDEALISM
MR. WADDINGTON OF WYCK
THE THREE SISTERS
THE RETURN OF THE PRODIGAL

A CURE OF SOULS

BY
MAY SINCLAIR

New York
THE MACMILLAN COMPANY
1924

All rights reserved

PRINTED IN THE UNITED STATES OF AMERICA

COPYRIGHT, 1924,

BY THE MACMILLAN COMPANY.

Set up and electrotyped.   Published January, 1924.

PR
6037
I73
C8

FERRIS PRINTING COMPANY
NEW YORK

A CURE OF SOULS

CHAPTER I

THE Reverend Canon Clement Purcell Chamberlain stood before the looking-glass brushing his hair. A pale vicuna dressing-gown, girdled and tasselled, sheathed him like a monk's frock. The shaven face between the oval yellow-backed twin brushes showed handsome, long and full, not too austerely Roman, red-brown, sleek with health. Young, too, for forty-three; only a few faint parallel lines across the forehead, crow's feet almost invisible about the eyes. Under the rhythmic strokes of the twin brushes the sleek brown hair fitted tight like a cap to the large head. It waved a little at the temples.

Through the open window an air smelling of lavender and warm roses blew on him.

He enjoyed the rhythm of the brushes, the cut of the stiff bristles through the hair and their scraping on the scalp. Once risen up out of his perfect bed, Canon Chamberlain enjoyed all the processes that prepared him for another

I

82545

blessed day: the hot bath, the sweet white lather polishing his white skin, the cold sponging after, the gymnastic exercises that gave him an agreeable sense of slenderness and fitness, taut, hard muscles working up through the almost imperceptible layer of fat; even shaving, once he had made up his mind to it, because it left your face so exquisitely clear and clean.

And now he was putting on the round collar, the high waistcoat, the short easy morning coat of black serge. A brief station at his pre-Dieu under the ivory Christ on his ebony cross; a slight tension of constraint, his attitude before the Immaterial; not so enjoyable as he made himself believe. But, like the discharge of any regular function, prayer gave relief.

He was now spiritually ready for his day.

The French windows of his dining-room stood wide open. The August morning, shining and scented, lured him outside. He passed from the green lawn through a tunnel of rose-trees to his kitchen garden. The flagged walks were warm and golden. Already on the southward wall the peaches gave out a sweet, hot smell. He liked to gather peaches straight from the wall, with the warmth of the sun on them, knowing that no hands but his had touched them. He liked to feel his teeth tearing the creamy peach-flesh from its crimson heart; to suck out of it the sweet-smelling juice. He ate two, nosing and fingering the velvet skin, before he peeled it. They were delicious. He took pleasure in the thought that peaches eaten before breakfast would be good . for him. A thrill of physical well-being went through him under the sleek, sun-warmed skin and in the running blood and quiet nerves.

He walked back, slowly, through the rose-tunnel, to his house. He loved every day the sight of the old Rectory, resting above its green lawns; gold-grey walls and mouse-grey roof; the straight lines of the dormer windows sloping to the eaves, and under them the two rows of square-browed mullioned windows, the lower row cut by the high glass doors of the dining-room. Resting in perfect peace. Enchanting smells met him as he entered, of hot coffee, of crisp bacon, of omelette. His breakfast.

Five letters lay with the *Morning Post* beside his plate there. He glanced at them uneasily, they might contain something disturbing to his perfect peace. In any case they would have to be answered. Better not open them till he had had his breakfast. He could see one from his sister, Charlotte Roper. Something disagreeable, you might be sure. He wasn't going to begin with Charlotte. Stay—that enormous envelope would be from Falconer, the sculptor, the estimate and design for the Queningford cum Kempston Maisey War Memorial. Nothing disturbing there. But he would have to think about it, and he didn't want to start his day thinking. Time enough when all his admirable digestive processes were complete.

He began with the omelette. Nobody like Fuller for making an omelette, always the same, neither too wet nor too dry, with a crisp curl at the edges and coloured golden. High wages, but he didn't grudge them to an excellence like Fuller's, and he could afford it. When all was said and done he could afford it. He meditated for a moment on the income he had at last acquired through the deaths of his elder brother and an uncle, ensuring to him forever the means of happy life. It had come to him so recently that he still thought of it with a sort of pious wonder. That it should have come at a time when taxation was so intolerably high showed clearly that the world was ruled by a benignant Providence. Goodness of God. And this new living too; one of the best in the diocese. To be sure there were things he wanted that he still had to do without; a butler who would also valet him, and an expert gardener for the fruit and vegetables. If he had not subscribed so largely to the War Memorial—— And in a large, scattered parish like Queningford cum Kempston Maisey a motor car and a chauffeur were a necessity. No comfort in driving himself about in a cramped little governess cart.

It would be awful if Fuller were to leave him. He must raise her wages next quarter, must manage it somehow. A woman who could make an omelette like that. And coffee. Coffee and omelettes and novels. They did them best in France. Nothing finer than a good French novel.

He wondered what the hotels were like in the Riviera now. The Californie at Cannes in nineteen-eleven. Ah, that was a holiday. He could see the great dining-room, blond in the sunlight, the little tables. And the food. It couldn't be the same now, since the war. He wondered what France was going to do about those reparations. There was no doubt that Germany could pay if proper pressure were brought to bear. Expert's opinion. He opened his *Morning Post* to see what France was going to do. And Lloyd George. If only you could trust Lloyd George. But he didn't trust him for one minute. He didn't trust the Coalition. What a Government to have to pray for every Sunday. "That Thou would'st be pleased to direct and prosper all their consultations." . . . If you could pray for the collapse of the Coalition, now, and the establishment of a sound Tory Government, a party government, with the responsibility of party. Pity that the Church had no longer any hand in the affairs of State. If one could but make Christianity a living force in politics. But Lloyd George was a dissenter. What could you expect?

The *Morning Post* tided him over to toast and marmalade. Fuller again. Was there anything that woman couldn't do?

Yes. He would certainly eat two peaches before breakfast every morning, as long as they lasted. If young Jackman ate two peaches every morning before breakfast he would get through his work better and not write such dull sermons. He must tell him. No, better not. If he went about preaching peaches he would feel morally bound to make presents of the fruit. He must have another bit of butter to finish that marmalade. And honey. He must tell

Fuller to order some honey at Parker's. They had some, very clear and beautiful, in jars.

The meal was over. Canon Chamberlain rejoiced once more in the perfect working of his organism. The sense of fitness exalted him like a gentle beatitude. For one moment he stood outside on the flagged walk and let the sun soak into him; then he returned, took up his letters and withdrew into the deep peace of his study. Sunshine and the smell of lavender and roses streamed into it from the garden. It was lined with books; burnished leather and gilt tooling and the bright edges of furniture caught the light. The place shone and was soundless. No bed was more restful than those deep claret coloured leather armchairs. He knew where the French novels were, there on the bottom shelf, hidden behind the short green curtain: Dumas and Balzac, Flaubert and Maupassant and Anatole France. Nobody like them. Presently, when the business of the morning was over he would take up one of them and settle down in his armchair for the rest of the morning. In the afternoon he might go over to Kempston Maisey and call on Mrs. Hancock. Or he might not. He might settle down again in the cool under the beech-tree. He had a voluptuous satisfaction in the thought that he might or might not call on that delightful woman. Nothing constrained him and the alternative was delightful, too.

A dim uneasiness came over him. Not worry, but the flying shadow of worry, the ghostly premonition of something unpleasant. Charlotte's letter. Supposing Charlotte had written to ask if she and Daphne could come and stay with him?

He would deal with Charlotte's letter first and get it over.

N-no. He couldn't say that Charlotte had asked him in so many words. But she had said she didn't know where on earth she was to take Daphne for her holiday this August. She had said they were sick of the sea-side. She had said she supposed he had fairly settled down in Queningford by this time and she would like to see the Rectory some day. She had said it sounded charming. And if that wasn't a broad hint, what was it? He hated people who gave hints.

Luckily Charlotte didn't know how charming the Rectory was. And Queningford. She didn't realise Sir Charles and Lady Sarah Philpot at the Manor and their three unmarried sons. She didn't realise the two young curates, Mr. Jackman and Mr. Cartwright. If Charlotte had, if she once began to look on Queningford Rectory as a matrimonial centre for Daphne he would never have her out of the house. And Charlotte's presence for longer than, say, a fortnight at the outside, was in the highest degree undesirable. For Charlotte possessed a perfect genius for unpleasantness. Not only did she draw attention to anything disagreeable that might be happening in your neighbourhood, she raked up the forgotten past, she reminded you of everything disagreeable that had ever happened or was about to happen. She had an unholy insight into all intimate, fugitive and secret things; other people's motives, for example. Nothing was hidden from Charlotte. Her brutal criticism and Daphne's violent high spirits were destruction to your peace. The ways of peace have they not known. He couldn't bear it if they acquired the habit of staying at the Rectory.

They must not find Queningford too charming. It was a good thing, after all, he hadn't got a motor car. A motor car would have been an irresistible attraction to Charlotte and Daphne. When he thought of Charlotte and

Daphne he could almost have been sorry that Fuller was so good a cook. He must not ask them now when the Philpots were at home and the tennis parties and picnics and peaches were on. He would ask them in October when the Philpots would be away in London and the tennis parties and picnics and peaches would be over, and he would tell them that Queningford was the dullest place on earth.

He would sit down and write to Charlotte now and invite her for the middle of October. He would say that he would not be free from tiresome parish work till then. As Charlotte might imagine, the complete reorganization of work, in a parish that had been allowed to go to rack and ruin, took up every minute of his day. And he warned her, they would find it very dull.

Two other letters were less perturbing. One was from Miss Lambert who, in accordance with his kind suggestion, would be at the Rectory tomorrow morning at eleven. One was from Miss Hilda Wrinch to the same effect. Miss Lambert realised fully the weight of his engagements and hoped that among them they would be able to arrange the parish work so as to relieve him of the greater burden. Miss

Hilda Wrinch didn't see where *she* came in, but if he wanted his parish magazines hawked about the country, she could manage that all right on her motor bike. But call on villagers who didn't want to be called on, or teach in the Sunday school she would *not*.

Canon Chamberlain smiled. All his sympathies were with Miss Wrinch; he, too, objected to poking his nose into places where he wasn't wanted, especially when the places didn't smell nice, and they seldom did.

The other letter was from Sir Charles Philpot, who wrote that he heartily approved of the Rector's plans for the War Memorial. He could think of no place for it more suitable than our beautiful old Parish Church, and he agreed that the Nonconformists, cutting themselves off from the rest of the religious community, had no claim to be consulted in the matter.

Canon Chamberlain felt that his hands were considerably strengthened by this backing from Sir Charles.

For there had been a painful division in his committee, some well-meaning but misguided members holding that a War Memorial belonged to the townspeople and should stand in the market place, while the Rector and the Squire maintained that the only possible position was inside the consecrated shelter of the Parish Church. When Dr. Lawson submitted that it was undesirable to offend all the Nonconformists in Queningford, the Rector replied with appropriate irony. Did Dr. Lawson suggest that the Memorial should be set up in the Baptist Chapel, and, if not, there was only one question for the Committee—Was a War Memorial a sacred or a secular object? If a secular object, let it stand in the market place by all means. But he believed that nobody present would deny that the War Memorial, their tribute to their beloved dead, was most peculiarly sacred, and if so, there was no fitting place of honour for it outside the Parish Church.

And as the Rector and the Squire had each contributed ten times as much as the two biggest subscribers taken together and a hundred times more than most of them, if any one scheme was entitled to consideration it was theirs. So the Rector's and the Squire's scheme carried the day. The comments of the townspeople came too late, besides being mostly private, uttered behind shop counters and in little parlours and in bars. And when the Baptist minister, deeply moved, sent a letter of protest

to Canon Chamberlain, the rector, replying,
turned a sentence very delicately to the effect
that Nonconformity was Nonconformity, and
that Mr. Binns should have weighed the consequences before he turned his back and the backs
of his congregation on communion with the
Church. At the same time Canon Chamberlain felt more than ever at this moment that
the tragedy of the war, falling upon all alike,
united all in one communion of sorrow. He,
personally, laid aside all differences of denomi-
nation, and Mr. Binns might rest assured that
every Baptist in Queningford would be cordially
welcome to enter the church at any hour, save
only during Divine Service, and lay his or her
flowers on the Memorial. A suitable slab would
be provided for this purpose. He almost made it
appear that the slab had been provided out of
special consideration for the Baptists. At the
same time he was vaguely aware that the emotions of the townspeople were against his
scheme, so that Sir Charles's support was peculiarly gratifying. He wrote and said that Sir
Charles had strengthened his hands.

There remained Falconer's estimate and design for the Memorial. Nothing to worry him
there. Falconer's estimate was reasonable and

his design in strict accordance with the instruc-
tions given him by the Rector. A tablet engraved with the names of the men who had fallen, under a shallow, pointed canopy, decorated
Gothic of the Fifteenth Century. For the Parish Church was all beautifully in its period, and
if the War Memorial was to be admitted it must
do no violence to the Parish Church.

He wrote to Falconer accepting his estimate
and design (the committee had very properly
left it to him) ; and then he dismissed the War
Memorial from his mind. He didn't want to
think about the War Memorial; he didn't want
to think about the War and about the young
men who had fallen in it. These things were
very disturbing to his state of gentle beatitude.
He wanted to sit in his armchair and smoke
cigarettes and read *Madame Bovary*; which he
did. He disapproved of Flaubert, and enjoyed
him. Disapproved so thoroughly that, review-
ing the famous trial, his sympathies were all
' with the prosecution. He felt that his disap-
proval consecrated his enjoyment. Besides, he
was safe. A man was a fool if at forty-three
he had acquired no knowledge of himself. He
had the just measure of his own integrity, and
could trust it. Sane mind in sane body, invul-

nerable, immune. Apostolic immunity. If they drink any deadly thing it shall not hurt them. And to the pure——

Still he had compassion on his weaker brother, on breakable, perishable innocence, and Flaubert and Maupassant were popped behind the green curtain after every sitting.

The morning moved on slowly to one o'clock. Luncheon came with the odour of lamb's cutlets, breaded. (Fuller's luncheons were as perfect as her breakfasts, if you could compare luncheon with breakfast, or noon with the freshness of the morning.)

After coffee the Rector sat in his armchair in that blessed state which is neither sleep nor waking, but a voluptuous, dreamless sinking into peace, a foretasting of sleep, an exquisite saturation.

He was roused by the sound of the church bell tolling. Old Trinder's funeral. Jackman was taking it. He had no high opinion of the senior curate, but Jackman had his uses. He could take funerals. The Rector's peace was deepened by the thought that Jackman, not he, would be out there in the blazing sun, without a hat, taking Trinder's funeral. If Trinder had been an important parishioner he would have had to take it himself. Mercifully, important parishioners very seldom died.

The bell went on tolling, tolling, from the high church tower, beating the golden crystal air, first the clanging of iron, then a ringing like wires, then a crystalline vibration, singing like thin glass. Between each stroke he slid again, voluptuously, towards sleep.

Three o'clock. Old Trinder was buried. He wouldn't have to call any more at the cottage by the river, smelling of damp and sickness. One more disagreeable duty done with forever. He put this thought away from him and said to himself that, if old Trinder wasn't important, he was a good man, a just man. He was sorry that Trinder was dead, and that he would never see him again slipping forward on his hard wooden chair, never hear his voice, strangled by the hawking, rattling cough.

Ah well, he had sent poor old Trinder all the soup he wanted. You might say Trinder had been kept alive by the soup he had sent him.

That was the half hour. If he was going to Kempston to call on Mrs. Hancock, he would have to go. But he was aware, deliciously aware, that he was not going to call on Mrs. Hancock. It was much too hot. He would call tomorrow. He could then look forward to Mrs. Hancock all today.

And he settled down in the cool under the beech-tree with *Madame Bovary*. Gladys, the parlourmaid, punctual, smiling Gladys, moving softly, clipped in her black and white, with a face pure and open as a flower, Gladys brought him his tea there. When he saw it coming a little fear stirred in him uneasily. Supposing Mr. Cartwright or Mr. Jackman were to drop in. Cartwright so boisterous, is enthusiastic and is fatiguing, and Jackman so depressed that he seemed to be forever taking somebody's funeral.

But they did not drop in. Nothing, absolutely nothing happened to disturb his matchless ease. And the day moved on, calm, unhurrying, to dinner time. Fuller surpassed herself. Positively he must raise her wages. He would raise them next month.

Calm and unhurrying, the evening moved on to bed-time. •The Canon knelt again at his prie-Dieu, constrained, glad to get his prayer over. He stretched himself in his perfect bed, supported by the buoyancy of the high spring mattress. He slept. He dreamed of being too late for Sir Charles Philpot's funeral, and woke again to another blessed day.

CHAPTER II

IF only today could be as yesterday.

But it was not. The trouble began early in the morning when he had hardly finished breakfast. He hated people who called early in the morning, interfering with the serene, leisured course of his digestion. Dr. Lawson, too, who ought to have known better. Gladys should have known better than to have let him in.

The doctor had called about the War Memorial. He hoped that Canon Chamberlain would see his way to reconsidering his decision. And as Canon Chamberlain had dismissed the War Memorial from his mind yesterday he was in no mood for considering it at all today. As for going back on his decision, that was out of the question. The matter had been settled in committee. And Falconer had the commission. The design was chosen: a tablet engraved with the men's names, under a Fifteenth Century canopy. That, he said, would harmonize with the church's period.

"But," said Dr. Lawson, "it won't harmonise with the general feeling. The general feeling is that a simple cross or obelisk, set up in the market place, where it can be seen by everybody coming and going, and where the villagers can lay their flowers——"

"The Memorial can be seen in the church, and the villagers can lay their flowers on the slab provided for the purpose."

"It isn't the same thing at all. The feeling is that a memorial in the market place would be *their* memorial and that a memorial in your church would be *yours*."

The young man was dark and hard and shrewd, and he looked at Canon Chamberlain as if he knew what was the matter with him.

"It's as much their church as mine."

"You can't say it's the Nonconformists' church. The Nonconformists have given their sons to the country, too."

"The names of the Nonconformists' sons will be on the tablet. I make no distinction."

"I should hope you didn't. But consider the feelings of their families. If those poor people want to bring their flowers and wreaths and things, they must bring them into your church."

"Not my church, God's church."

"God's church, then, and they're there on sufferance. They'll know they're there on sufferance and they won't like it."

"They know they are welcome. I've written to Mr. Binns to tell him so."

"Precisely. Mr. Binns and Mr. Binns's congregation have to get your permission. Don't you see that the whole thing's being taken from the townspeople and hidden away in your church?"

The Canon made another movement of deprecation, but Dr. Lawson disregarded the gesture and went on.

"Hidden away in your church as if it didn't belong to them. It's your show, not theirs. You've simply scooped it for your church and the glory of it."

Again he fixed him with those hard, shrewd eyes, his pitiless diagnosis.

"Honestly," he said, "that's what it looks like to them. And hang it all, they've subscribed to the blessed thing."

"I'm afraid, Dr. Lawson, it is quite impossible for us to see eye to eye in this matter. You are not a churchman."

"I'm not a Nonconformist, either."

"I suppose you are what you'd call an agnostic. Well, I've every sympathy with honest doubt. Shows that you've thought about religion. But I must protest against this attitude of hostility. *I* have no attitude of hostility."

"It isn't hostility to *you*, sir."

"Hostility to what I stand for. That's worse."

"No. I'm simply expressing the general feeling. If you'd lost a son in the war, how would you like it if you had to take your flowers to the Baptist chapel at Mr. Binns's invitation?"

"It isn't the same thing at all," said the Canon in his turn.

"It seems to me precisely the same thing."

"The Baptist's chapel the same thing as the Church of England? Really, Dr. Lawson, I cannot discuss the matter with you on that basis. Why discuss at all when we've no common ground of argument?"

"I should have thought the feeling of the village was common ground enough."

"You talk as if I were outraging the feeling of the village, as if I were dishonouring the dead. You don't seem able to understand that their glory *is* the Church's glory, and that the Church is paying them the very highest honour in taking their glory to herself, as you put it.

They are her sons, even if they've disowned and left her."

"That doesn't meet the case of the Nonconformists."

"It meets all cases. The Nonconformists have only themselves to thank if they feel they've been left out in the cold."

"You admit, then, that you've left them out?"

"I admit nothing of the sort. I've given them the most cordial invitation to come in."

"That's my whole point. They don't *want* your invitations. They want the right to honour their dead in their own place and their own way. And your scheme robs them of their right. I do think it is a case when the really fine thing would have been to give way, not to force your scheme."

"My scheme was approved by a majority of the committee."

"Oh yes, I daresay you and Philpot contrived to make them toe the line, between you. The tradespeople daren't stand up to the rector and the squire. But you should hear how they go on behind your back."

"I must decline," said the Rector, "to argue the question any further."

"All right, sir, I've said my say. I'm sorry I must withdraw my subscription."

"Thank you. The response has already been so generous that your subscription will not be needed. It's your own loss, Dr. Lawson."

Surely, he thought, he must be aware that Sir Charles and I gave a hundred each, and he talks about withdrawing his five guineas. Well, I've shown him pretty plainly that we're not going to be brow-beaten by him. Nor by Mr. Binns, either.

He held himself very stiff and straight. But the interview had upset him all the same. The doctor's queer eyes had affected him very disagreeably. He had an uncomfortable suspicion that his motives might not, after all, have been so very pure. He *had* wanted his own way. He had forced his scheme on his committee against the feeling of the townspeople. He had bought acquiescence with the sheer weight of his subscription and his clerical prestige. Well, and why not? He *was* the rector of the parish. The War Memorial *was* a sacred object, and the Church was interested, as no secular authority could be, in its site. The Church was above the village, above the country, it was above everything. These Queningford men who died for the country had died far more for Christianity and the Church. He really felt that if their glory was not the Church's glory they had died in vain. It might be true that he wanted to identify the Memorial with himself or himself with the Memorial; but it was not true, what that fellow Lawson had insinuated, that he was taking their glory to himself. How *could* he take their glory to himself?

At the same time he had a vision of that other War Memorial, the slender shaft of the cross set up in the middle of the market place, the broad round base where the villagers could lay their flowers, the tall cross that they would see every day, coming and going, they could see it from their windows, they could feel that it was theirs. They could meet round it without distinction of class or sect or creed. He had once seen an old stone cross on Dartmoor, standing on the edge of a field. Sheep couched round it, huddled close to the foot of the cross. He could see their helpless, innocent backs blurred and grey in the twilight. The sight had stirred in him some secret, poignant sense of poetry. He remembered it now. And they shall be one fold under one shepherd.

But no. The War Memorial was a sacred

object. Its place was in the Parish Church. A shallow shrine, decorated Gothic of the Fifteenth Century. All in the period. He had seen to that.

CHAPTER III

ELEVEN o'clock. The Rector took up a position in his drawing-room, his beautiful drawing-room, all shining gold-brown Chippendale, flowery cretonne and Lowestoft china, with deep-cushioned chairs and couches, and old rose curtains fading in the southern light. He liked to receive women in his drawing-room, it was so perfect that it defied their approaches delicately; it seemed to say that all this refinement and this comfort had been achieved without feminine assistance; it was finished; it waited for no woman's hand. It intimated in the gentlest possible manner that the Rector was happy in his state of celibacy. He was sufficient to himself.

The smile the Rector had for them was a smile of genial immunity. It flattered them, but not too much. It didn't pay them the homage of embarassment. He had none of the shy awkwardness of conscious sex. He was sure of himself but without fatuity. His worst enemy couldn't say that he was fatuous. Charlotte had not said it.

It was with this handsome smile, showing square white teeth and ending at his teeth, leaving his eyes unlighted, that he came forward to Miss Lambert and Miss Wrinch.

"How kind of you," he said. "And what charming punctuality."

"We are not too soon?" Miss Lambert said.

She was the gentlest woman, he thought, that he had ever seen. Not young, forty-five, perhaps, graceful and slender. She had a small, tenderly inquisitive face, with a thin waving mouth, a thought too wide for it. A few shallow lines of middle-age were flooded and effaced with a pink flush. Light brown hair, striped with grey, went waving, too, under her melancholy hat. From the black brim her dark blue eyes looked out at you with a sort of sadness and wonder.

"Fragile," he meditated, and the thought disturbed him. For his comfort in the parish would depend largely on the amount of work he could get out of Miss Lambert. Fragile, and forty-five, if a day.

Thus he appraised her.

"You couldn't come too soon," he replied with chivalrous mendacity.

"*I* came soon," Miss Wrinch announced, "because I've got to go soon."

Almost he could have sworn that a light came into Miss Lambert's eyes when she heard Miss Wrinch saying she had got to go.

For his own part he didn't care how soon Miss Wrinch went. Tall and robust, standing like a man, in breeches and belted overall, with a boy's impudent face in short swinging hair, shouting in that deep boy's voice, Hilda Wrinch jarred on his nerves. They had been already tormented sufficiently by Dr. Lawson. She produced much the same effect on him as young Cartwright, his junior curate of Kempston Maisey, with his boisterous energy. He judged her obstinate as a mule, a girl who would turn the parish upside down to get her own way. And yet so robust, so energetic that, if he could only handle her, she might prove extremely useful, she and her motor bike.

He said it was a pity she had got to go soon, but if that was so, perhaps Miss Lambert would forgive them if they discussed her business first.

"Oh, *my* business won't take long. What do

you want me to do? I can't do *much,* you know."

"You suggested very kindly that you would distribute the Parish Magazine."

"Where?"

"Well, in Queningford and Kempston. And —er—the outlying cottages and farms."

"Outlying as much as you like. Anywhere I can get to on my motor bike. I can be all over the place in a jiffy. But I don't see myself foot-slogging round the village, thumping at every door."

"Well, but the magazine's got to be left at the subscribers. They *do* subscribe, you know."

Miss Wrinch stood firm.

"I can't help that," she said.

"But, dear me, what am I to do?"

"You visit 'em, don't you?"

"Yes. Yes. Of course I—I visit them."

"Well then, can't you just dump the thing down on them as you go?"

His heart sank. *He* was expected to distribute his own parish magazine, was he? What then were curates and what were district visitors for?

"Is there no one in this village who is willing to help? How about Miss Minchin?"

Miss Lambert smiled, a smile of great sweetness and holiness.

"I think we can manage without troubling either Miss Minchin or the Rector. If you, Hilda, will take Kempston and the distant subscribers, I will do the 'foot-slogging and thumping.' It will be all in the day's work."

"That doesn't seem fair.

"What is Miss Minchin doing, and why is she not here?" said the Rector.

"Miss Minchin has given up her district. She thinks she has enough to do with Miss Wrinch's Girls' Club and the Mothers' Meetings."

"Given up her district, and who is taking it on?"

"I am," said Miss Lambert.

"In addition to your own?"

"In addition to my own."

"Is that right? You look, if I may say so, hardly strong enough——"

"I am very strong, very wiry. I was deaconness of St. Saviour's, Southwark, when I was in London. This," said Miss Lambert, "is nothing."

Miss Wrinch was holding out her large, powerful hand.

"Well, I'm off. I say, you don't want **me to**
go in and sit with them, do you?"

"Now and then it would be kind."

"Kind? Some of them haven't seen my mug
before and don't want to see it."

"You must feel your way. Use tact. I shall
want you to report any cases of sickness or
distress——"

"Oh well—*that*—if the poor beggars are ill,
of course. But look here, if I do this for you,
you'll look in now and then at my Girls' Club?
We're just starting. Come tomorrow night and
give us a good send-off."

"Really, I should have thought my presence
was hardly necessary."

"Oh, isn't it! If you want 'em to love you."

Did he? Did he want them to love him?
Didn't he want before everything to be let
alone? And what would Queningford do with
a Girls' Club? At this rate he would soon have
more to do, not less.

"Come," said Miss Wrinch, "I'm not going
to let you off as easy as all that. What's a half
hour at my Club compared with my biking for
miles round the country with your parish magazine?"

"Really, Hilda——" Miss Lambert's face

seemed to say "Do you hear her, this wild girl? Do you want anything so irresponsible?"

Miss Wrinch, poised on one foot, waited.

"Are you coming or are you not? A bargain's a bargain."

"Very well. *Very* well. I'll come. Tomorrow evening, is it?"

"Tomorrow evening. Any time between eight and ten. Right-oh!"

And presently Miss Wrinch and her motor bike disappeared round the turn of the drive in a fury of explosions. He could hear the honk-honk of her horn as she rushed through the market place.

"And now, my dear Miss Lambert, I think you would find this armchair more comfortable."

Miss Lambert, very straight on an austere Chippendale, protested. He was firm. She at last consented, sitting up among the cushions with her curious stiff grace, a middle-aged Madonna with empty arms. He put more cushions at her back, and a footstool at her feet. He had the air of cherishing her. A woman who was prepared to work for him like a deaconess in Southwark was worth cherishing. Besides, people sitting uncomfortably made him feel uncomfortable.

He began to wonder why the two other district visitors had not appeared.

"Now," he said, "for the Sunday school—what names have we?"

"Mrs. Dancy, Mrs. Caldecott, Mrs. Ballinger, Miss Minchin, and the two Kimbers for the younger classes. Mr. Jackman for the big boys."

"And for the big girls?"

"Me," said Miss Lambert.

"And the Superintendent?"

"Me," said Miss Lambert again.

"Good." No need for him to look in if he didn't want to.

At this moment Gladys came in with two notes on a tray. From the district visitors who had not yet appeared.

"Forgive me, I think this is our business."

It was. Mrs. Lawson and Mrs. Caldecott both resigned their districts; the doctor's wife because her new baby absorbed all her time and attention, Mrs. Caldecott for no ostensible reason. But he knew that the War Memorial was at the bottom of these defections. Mrs. Lawson's name spoke for itself, baby or no baby;

Mrs. Caldecott had lost an only son in the war; and the Lawsons and the Caldecotts were as thick as thieves.

"This is unfortunate. I see no earthly excuse for Mrs. Caldecott, a woman with nothing in the world to do."

Miss Lambert was silent. She looked pained and embarrassed, as if she knew why Mrs. Caldecott had deserted.

"I don't know what we're to do. I can think of nobody to fill their places."

"There is I," said Miss Lambert.

"My dear lady, you can't take on the whole village."

"I can. The whole village is child's play after Southwark. You forget this is my life-work. I wish to devote myself entirely to it."

"And who is to take the Mothers' meetings?"

"I," said Miss Lambert.

"And the Coal and Blanket Club?"

"I."

"You are too good."

"No. No." Her flush deepened. "Really, Canon Chamberlain, I had rather do all the work myself than delegate any of it. Then I know that it will be done thoroughly. I know where I am. It saves friction——"

(And he hated friction.)

"If you only knew the difficulties, the petty jealousies one meets when one has to work with village people, you'd understand."

He seemed to ponder it, to hesitate.

"Really, you may depend on me. I shall make it my pleasure to work in with you, to meet all your wishes. I can promise that you will have less and not more to think of in the future."

"You are *very* good——"

"Oh, no. Not good. I should be ashamed if I did less than my utmost. You never spare yourself, why should I spare myself? Only trust me——"

He looked at her and saw her face lit up, exalted. He knew what he had to deal with, a woman devoted to the last extremity; a woman with a sacred vocation; a woman who would lift all burdens from his back. What could he have hoped for more?

"I do trust you." He said it with some emotion. "I know, as you know, that the work will be done thoroughly. As thoroughly as if I did it myself."

He paused, gathering weight.

"I cannot tell you how I appreciate your decision. I was told this morning I should meet with opposition and ill-feeling. And I find co-operation and good-will."

"You mean," she said gently, "the Memorial."

"I mean the Memorial. They tell me——"

"Don't listen to them." She rose, more than ever exalted. "They don't know what they're talking about. They can't see—— How should they? Before you came there was nobody to make them see. Nobody cared. . . . If I might tell you how deeply I admire your plan for the Memorial. There is *no* place for it but the Church. You thought, did you not, of the Church gathering their names together, as she gathers their souls, sheltering, keeping watch over them——?"

"Yes. That was what I thought of."

"You were wonderful. These poor things will see it, they will understand some day. When they get used to it."

She held out her hand. He took it, pressed it. She withdrew it suddenly.

"Thank you, thank you, Miss Lambert," he said. "I see *you* understand me."

He added that she had strengthened his hands.

CHAPTER IV

HE couldn't settle down into his usual doze after luncheon, so he strolled into the kitchen garden to see how the peas and the cucumbers were getting on, and what peaches, if any, he could spare for Mrs. Hancock.

Positively he must call on her that afternoon.

The peas were getting on splendidly, the cucumbers were lengthening and swelling under the hot glass, and so many more peaches had ripened in yesterday's sun that a small basketful for Mrs. Hancock would be hardly missed. He pinched them gently, testing their ripeness, marking down several very fine ones for Mrs. Hancock.

He had begun a dessert of peaches from the wall when he saw Gladys hurrying towards him down the garden walk. He disliked all the appearances of hurry, most particularly he disliked to be caught eating peaches in an uncivilised manner. From the look on the girl's face he divined a visitor. Gladys, in sheer irresponsible, thoughtless levity, was smiling.

"Mr. Cartwright to see you, sir."

Cartwright was the last person he desired to see or be seen by. A rector's life was a dog's life, no peace from one minute to another.

"Where is he?"

"In the study, sir."

He paused, in an attitude of dignity, wiping his mouth and fingers, ceremonially, on his pocket handkerchief.

"Shall I show him out here, sir?"

"Yes——" Just in time he thought of his, of Mrs. Hancock's peaches; he had a vision of ravishment, Cartwright's unbridled youth. "No, I'll go to him."

Gladys smiled again, as if she knew, as if she had been teasing him by the suggestion.

Young Cartwright stood on the hearthrug, the hot image of impatience. His tall, broad body, tight muscles smoothing his black serge sleeves and trousers legs, his big head with the crisp, curling light-brown hair, his short high nose, his round, jutting chin and pushed-out mouth suggested a violent physical eagerness and energy. Drilled too, holding himself well, like a soldier, after five years in Kitchener's Army, and hardened by trench life. The curate's large face was still red with his three mile rush from Kempston

Maisey to Queningford; a pink cincture marked
his forehead. His round, clerical hat stood up
on its brim in a corner of the sofa, where he had
flung it as he took his stand. He was perspiring freely. It made you hot and uncomfortable
to look at him.

His face broke up into a sudden, large, shining smile. The Rector's hand was screwed in a
vigorous grip.

"Well, Cartwright, what's brought *you* over
in all this heat?"

"Oh, no end of things, sir."

He showed a disposition to remain standing,
as though he were too full of energy to sit down.

"Sit down. Sit down." The Rector was
seated, his left hand still nursing his tortured
right.

"Have you had lunch?" The question was
almost a rebuke.

"Yes, thanks. You don't mind my calling at
this time, do you? I knew I should find you at
home."

"Oh, no, my time is everybody's time. Have
you had coffee?"

No, Mr. Cartwright hadn't had coffee. He
had been too eager to be up and away, to catch
the Rector before he went out. He would be

glad of some. He sprang up and rang the bell vigorously. Its clamour tore throbbing through the still place, violating its stillness. Somehow the junior curate could never do things quietly like other people.

"Bless my soul, my dear boy, you'll bring the house down. What a Samson you are, Cartwright."

"Sorry, sir. Beastly row, I know."

"Well, what is it? Any more plans?"

"Rather."

The Rector's spirit shuddered as if down an invisible spine. If Cartwright had come to talk to him about his plans—It tired him already only to think about Cartwright's plans, to see him there, bursting with them, on a day like this.

"I thought you'd like to know how we're getting on at Kempston."

"Ah—how are you—er—getting on?"

"Top-hole, sir. There's hardly an empty sitting in the church. The Sunday school attendance is bigger than it was when you first came. We're getting the lads out of the public-houses. Mr. Thatcher tells me the very children in the day schools are brighter than they were. When you think of the slackness that's come over other villages since the war——"

"And what do you put it down to, this improvement?"

"Well——" He hesitated. Really, it was not for him to say. The young man's face was hotter, so modest was he, yet so conscious that the improvement was due to his own untiring energy, to the sheer, hard body and brain work he had put in. As for the Rector, he had hardly shown his nose in the place, except to call on Mrs. Hancock, or exchange an occasional service.

"I think, sir," said Cartwright, "we can put it down mostly to the Men's Club. Of course it's meant some stiff collar-work. A long, steady grind, raking the fellows in. You'd hardly believe me if I told you what it's meant."

"Yes, Cartwright, I do believe you."

He did believe him. He knew what Cartwright was. But oh, how it fatigued him to hear him talking about collar-work and long, steady grinds. And knowing what Cartwright was, he knew that he'd have *his* neck in the collar very shortly if he got his way. He wouldn't be surprised if Cartwright suggested that he should start a Men's Club in Queningford. And he was determined that Cartwright shouldn't get his way. He had Kempston to do what he

liked with. He might surely leave Queningford
alone.

The enthusiastic young man went on.

"But it's been worth it. More worth while
than anything else we could have done."

He said "we" generously, knowing well that
he had had to do it all alone.

The entrance of Gladys cut short his flight.
He drank his coffee in large gulps; no fine, lin-
gering appreciation of its flavour. And he began again.

"In fact, the Club has been such a success in
Kempston that Queningford ought really to start
one too."

"But there's nobody in Queningford who *can*
start it. Jackman's impossible. He's got no
initiative, no initiative at all."

"I know, sir. But he'd help to run the Club
all right if it was started for him."

"By whom?"

"Well, I thought that *you,* sir——"

"Really, Cartwright, I don't see my way. You
say yourself the labour is enormous. Am I to
go from house to house, beating up members?"

"Something like that, sir. Or you could work
up a committee."

"I've had enough of committees. They only

waste your time. You can talk for hours on end and not get any two persons to agree upon a plan. If you've got a plan yourself and try to carry it out you'll be at loggerheads with the lot of them. That at least has been my experience. I can't tell you the trouble I've had about this War Memorial, Cartwright."

"That's a different thing."

"Exactly. It isn't a secular thing. I was entirely within my rights. Yet they're all up against me. You might have thought I'd stolen the Memorial. Lawson was here this morning, pitching into me."

The curate was silent, so gravely silent that Canon Chamberlain wondered whether he didn't side, secretly, with his opponents. He had never known what Cartwright's point of view was. He was determined to get it out of him, whatever it might be.

"What do you think about it yourself?" he said.

"About the War Memorial?"

"About the site for the War Memorial."

"Do you really wish me to say, sir?"

"I've asked you. Are you with me or against me?"

"I didn't mean to say anything about it; but

if you insist, well, I do think it's a pity to offend so many good people."

"They've no business to be offended."

And he went over it again. The Memorial was a sacred object; the Church was doing honour to their dead; the Nonconformists had no claim, or shadow of claim; and all the rest of it. He spun it out, hoping thus to divert young Cartwright from his purpose.

"You don't agree?"

"I'm afraid not, sir."

"Well, I'm sorry you've joined the opposition. It isn't what I expected of you. Churchmen should stand shoulder to shoulder on a point like this. Our religion is a very sacred thing."

"To me, sir, *the* sacred thing is the feeling of all these people who've lost their nearest and dearest. It's religion in itself. But I haven't joined any opposition. If I heard a word against you, I should stand up for you."

"Would you, Cartwright?"

He was still playing for time, staving off the moment when Cartwright would return to his Club.

"Certainly. I'd have stuck the thing in the market place myself. But that's only my private feeling."

"Well—well—I must say you're very reasonable."

He paused. That pause was dangerous, but he had no more to say. Cartwright dashed into the opening.

"And about the Club, sir?"

The moment was not to be staved off any longer. Cartwright's persistence was abominable. And the Rector was beginning to feel the need of that doze after luncheon which he hadn't had.

A thought came to him. He could work the opposition against him so as to save himself.

"The Club——"

He seemed really to be considering it.

"You'll admit it's a good scheme?" said Cartwright.

"Excellent. Excellent scheme. But if you want it to succeed don't ask me to take it up. I'm an unpopular character at present."

"I don't think the feeling is personal. But if it were, wouldn't this be an opportunity to turn it? You'd be doing a really popular thing."

"My point is, Cartwright, that it wouldn't be a popular thing if I did it. The scheme would be damned—doomed from the beginning."

"I don't think so, sir. My belief is you'd win

'em all back. They'd see that you were identified with their interests."

The Rector meditated. Every way of escape seemed to be closed as soon as he turned down it. He must think of something else. But *what?*

Mr. Cartwright plunged on.

"You don't want Queningford to be behind Kempston."

"We are not so far behind. We've got our Girls' Club."

"Well, we shall have a Girls' Club in Kempston, too. That's another idea of mine—I mean of Miss Wrinch's. Splendid girl, Miss Wrinch. Magnificent energy. I wish we had her at Kempston."

"I wish you had."

"Oh, sir——"

"I mean Miss Wrinch is just a little *too* energetic, too boisterous, for my taste."

"Not boisterous. That's all on the surface. Good heart underneath. Keen—keen as mustard. She'll push anything through she turns her hand to."

Mr. Cartwright was doing himself no good. He was simply doubling his own disastrous effect by association with Miss Wrinch. They were, the Rector reflected bitterly, a pair of them.

Still, he saw his way out. Miss Wrinch was the gap for which, desperately, he made.

"Well," he said, "there you are. Miss Wrinch has started her Girls' Club without any help from me. It's up to the townspeople to start their own Men's Club. They'll value it ten times more if it *is* their own. Why can't they do what Miss Wrinch has done?"

"Because they're not Miss Wrinch. There isn't a man in the place who's capable of starting a Club. There wasn't one in Kempston. But they'll follow if you give them a lead."

"I doubt it."

"Look at Kempston."

"Yes. And it took you all your time. If it was stiff collarwork for you, Cartwright, what will it be for me?"

"But think, sir, of the difference between your position and your influence and mine."

He seemed almost to be saying, "Between your income and mine."

"My influence is very slight, considering my position."

"Oh no, sir, that isn't really so."

"Yes. Yes. We must look facts in the face. And as long as this ill-feeling lasts I'd rather not undertake any innovations in the village. After

all, how do we know that a Men's Club is
wanted? How do I know, if I started it tomorrow, that a single lad would turn up?"

"I can only say, sir, look at Kempston."

"Kempston isn't Queningford."

"No. It's smaller, even more primitive and
agricultural. Less likely. I'm sure that in
Queningford we should have a big response.
The men would turn up in scores."

"But would they keep on turning up? How
long has this Kempston affair been running? A
month?"

"Seven weeks. And we're emptying the public-houses."

"Seven weeks. Come to me in seven months'
time, and if your Club's still going strong, we'll
see about Queningford."

"I can answer for Kempston. And if we make
good you'll start a Club in Queningford?"

"I can't promise, Cartwright. I must see my
way here better than I see it now."

"Oh you'll see, sir. You'll see."

"I hope so." The Rector sighed his incredu-
lity. He had said his last word. He had staved
Cartwright off for another seven months, and he
now looked for him to go.

But Cartwright sat firm.

"The Kempston Club's a very small affair," he said. "But Queningford ought to make a big thing of it. You might rise to a reading-room and a billiard table. You could have smoking concerts, sing-songs, and lectures. With lantern slides. And there are people, like Lawson, who could read papers. You might get up debates. I'm starting a lending library at Kempston. And I've got other plans, too. I shall have a class for wood-carving in the winter and a class for boxing and drill. I'll have a fife and drum band before I've done. Drum them into church."

"My dear boy"—his head whirled with the mad rush of Cartwright's plans—"you won't have time to take the services at this rate."

"Oceans of time. Oceans of time. If you approve, I'm thinking of having a Service for Men Only on Sundays, at four o'clock. Half an hour's straight talk. The social evil and so on. A hymn or two and a prayer. If you approve——"

"I'm not sure that I do. I must think about it, Cartwright."

One thing was clear, that Cartwright meant him, too, to have a Service for Men Only, on Sundays, at four o'clock.

"I must think about it. It's a question whether these straight talks don't do more harm than good. Put ideas in the lads' heads."

"The ideas are there already. I want to take the wrong ones out and put the right ones in."

"Well, we must talk about it again."

"Very well, sir."

The Rector took out his watch and compared it with his clock.

"Ah, that clock is ten minutes slow. I thought so."

Young Cartwright took the hint.

"I must be going. Thank you most awfully for listening. I'm afraid I've taken up a terrible lot of your time."

"My time is more yours than mine. You are very welcome. But don't go too fast and don't have too many irons in the fire. *'Le mieux est l'ennemi du bien.'*"

"True. But we must get to the positive stage first, mustn't we?"

He was gone. But the air seemed to be ringing yet with his sound, his impact. Never, within fifty miles of Cartwright would he know peace. If only he could find a better curacy for Cartwright, or a living, a populous parish where his work would be cut out for him, where he wouldn't have to carve it, so to speak, out of other people's leisure.

He settled, sighing, into his armchair. He had still half an hour before he need start for Kempston. Perhaps if he read a little he might doze off. He took up *Madame Bovary*.

In ten minutes he was asleep.

CHAPTER V

GLADYS'S voice woke him suddenly.

"Mr. Jackman to see you, sir. In the drawing-room."

"Did you tell him I was going out?"

"Yes, sir, but he said he wouldn't keep you many minutes."

He wondered what on earth Jackman wanted to see him about. It might be to ask him whether his last sermon was too long, or whether he ought to remonstrate with Mrs. Filkins who had ceased to attend early celebration, or whether Mary Curtis, who had just had an illegitimate baby, was or was not entitled to the maternity bag. These were points that Jackman was never able to settle for himself. Or he might have come to discuss the War Memorial, with some ridiculous scruple about the Nonconformists; or for no reason except that he was feeling lonely and depressed and preferred tea at the Rectory to tea at his lodgings over the confectioner's shop. Next to Cartwright Mr. Jackman was the last person Canon Chamberlain wished to see. Yet he would have to see him, for there was always the off-chance that he had some really important matter to submit.

It was four o'clock and Canon Chamberlain decided that he would have tea first and drive over to Kempston afterwards when Mr. Jackman should have left him. The sooner Mr. Jackman had his tea the sooner he would go.

He found Mr. Jackman crushed into a chair in a posture of intense dejection. There was nothing especially alarming in that, since Mr. Jackman was habitually dejected, and though Canon Chamberlain disliked the young man's hang-dog air he had got used to it. The senior curate had gone through the war as a stretcher bearer in a field ambulance corps, and his experience had been, as he said, "shattering." Dark and lean, he had come out of it darker and leaner, with nervous gestures and a face stained a morbid sallow and scored with deep, sagging lines. One of these lines, drawn from his left nostril to his chin, twitched when you looked at him, jerking back his cheek with a clock-work movement which the Rector found very disagreeable. He had got into the way of not looking at Jackman in the hope of stopping it.

He was twitching now as he rose, holding out his long slender hand damp with sweat. (Another unpleasant peculiarity of Jackman's.) And he had been thrusting his fingers through his hair, raising a short, dry scrub. The Rector marked this sign of agitation with misgiving.

But as if he had only dropped in for tea, innocently, Mr. Jackman hung fire, uttering platitudes about old Trinder and the funeral and the sadness of Trinder's life that had been all loneliness and liver. Then, choosing the moment when the Rector had got his teeth into the first hot, rich slice of buttered crumpet, he let himself go.

"I've got something to tell you, sir."

He paused. He seemed to be swallowing something, something that was not tea, or crumpet; a fear, a scruple.

"Something disagreeable?"

"I'm afraid you'll consider it disagreeable."

"I know. It's the War Memorial. You can't tell me anything about the War Memorial I don't know."

"It isn't the War Memorial."

"Then it's Mary Curtis. She's had another illegitimate baby. You can't tell me anything about Mary Curtis I don't know."

"It isn't Mary Curtis. It's much worse. . . ."

Again he swallowed his invisible bitterness.

"Come, Jackman, what is it?"

"It's *me*."

He paused to let the awfulness of it sink into the Rector.

"Why," said the Rector cheerfully, "what's wrong with you?"

"Everything's wrong. My mind's wrong. I'm worried to death and I can't sleep."

"Ah—that's bad."

"I wouldn't mind that if I could see my way. But I can't see it. . . . I wonder, sir, if you could make me see?"

"Well, Jackman, I don't know. It depends on what the trouble is. You don't mean that—that you're in love?"

"I do not, sir. I wouldn't come and bother you with that sort of thing."

"Well, if you had I daresay I could have given you advice. You're letting your crumpet get cold."

The Rector had been annoyed at the sight of Jackman's damp hand hovering above the crumpets; he was still more annoyed to see that he had allowed his piece to lie congealed and revolting on his plate. It argued a mental disturbance that reflected unpleasantly on his own comfortable appetite. What had possessed Jackman to call at tea-time in this awful mood?

"Eat a good tea, Jackman. You'll feel better, and we can thrash it out quietly afterwards."

If only he would leave him in peace for this moment of tea-time.

The young man drank a little tea obediently and then stopped as if it had choked him. He rose and stood up awkwardly, holding his cup and saucer at a dangerous angle.

The Rector thought: In another minute he'll spill his tea and ruin my best Bokhara rug. And he'll smash that cup, too.

Bokhara rugs and Spode china didn't exist for Mr. Jackman in his mood. He didn't care what became of them. The Rector rose and took his cup from him and insisted on his sitting down.

"Now then," he said, "we can talk comfortably." He helped himself to another bit of buttered crumpet. He had filled the slop-bowl with boiling water and set the crumpets on the top to keep them hot. "What do you say the trouble is?"

"The trouble is that I can no longer believe what I used to believe."

"Doubts, Jackman?" He didn't want to listen

to Jackman's doubts. He wanted to sit and eat hot buttered crumpet in peace. "You're too old for that sort of thing. You should have got over all that at Cambridge in your first year."

"It didn't occur to me in my first year."

"Come, is it intellectual doubt that's worrying you?"

"All kinds of doubt, sir."

"Let's take them one at a time. The evidences, now. Are you shaky about the evidences, the authenticity of the historical books?"

"They seem to me, sir, comparatively unimportant."

"But they are most important. If you go deep enough into the question of the evidences, you will find that, though some books of the Old Testament may be suspect, the authenticity of the Gospels is established beyond controversy. Beyond controversy. If we take Galatians as the earliest of St. Paul's epistles, and we certainly may, we come down to within a few years, I forget the precise number of years, but at any rate a very few years of Christ's death and resurrection. We have St. Paul speaking with eye-witnesses. Eye-witnesses. You should read what Lightfoot has to say. There's a passage in Eusebius, quoting Papias, which settles the ques-

tion of St. John's Gospel. No reasonable person——"

The Rector had not considered the question
since some time in the nineties, and Lightfoot
seemed to him unanswerable. Now he came to
think of it, Lightfoot's point was not so much
what Eusebius said as what he didn't say, prov-
ing that what Eusebius did not mention was such
an obvious fact that there was no need to mention it.

"If I had Lightfoot I could lay my hands on
the passage——"

But Mr. Jackman waved Lightfoot away. It
was nothing to him what Eusebius said that
Papias said.

"Don't bother, sir. That isn't what worries
me. It is that I do not, I cannot believe any
longer in God—in the existence of God."

The Rector left off eating crumpet. He had
not anticipated anything so serious as this. It
might lead them anywhere. Into metaphysical
abysses. And why choose tea-time? It was too
bad of Jackman. Here was he, tired, wanting
nothing but to be left to finish his tea in peace,
and there was Jackman, huddled in his chair in
an attitude of unimaginable discomfort and saying that he didn't believe in God.

"Bless me, why not?"

"Because I do not and will not believe in an immoral God, and I see no evidence of any other."

This was terrible. Jackman could not have started a topic more subversive of all peace. He almost hated Jackman.

"My dear fellow, if you're going to knock your head against the moral problem at this time of day——"

"But it's at this time of day it's become so awful, sir. Before the war it never occurred to me to question God's wisdom. Or his power. Or his goodness. And now, if he exists at all and is the ruler of this world, I must deny that he is wise or all-powerful or good. He can't be all three."

"But, my dear boy, there have been wars since the world began, and there have been plagues and earthquakes, and yet men have believed in God."

"Because they didn't think, sir, or because they weren't mixed up in them. And if there have been plagues and earthquakes and other wars, that only makes his responsibility the greater. If he exists, and I prefer to think he doesn't. And there never was a war as awful as this war.

As if he'd tried to surpass himself, to surpass all his abominations."

"My dear Jackman, if I took you seriously I should say you were blaspheming. I do say you exaggerate."

"Exaggerate? You can't exaggerate the horror of this war. You can pile on all the horrors you know or can imagine, and you won't be anywhere near it. If you'd been through it, sir, if you'd seen the things that I've seen, and I haven't seen the worst. I hadn't got to fight and kill——"

"Yes, I can understand that you were very greatly upset, but it doesn't seem to me a reason for parting with your faith. After all, you must remember what that faith was to you."

"I do remember. That's what makes it hell. Some men take to unbelief gladly because of the intellectual relief it is; but to me it's torture; it's horrible; it's the loss of everything I care for most. I tell you I can't sleep at night. I *want* my God. And he isn't there. He never will be."

The Rector was feeling more and more uncomfortable. He was miserable in the presence of emotion. He always felt that there was something indecent about it. It was awful to see

Jackman writhing, perspiring, not with the heat
like Cartwright, but in his soul's agony. And
the crumpets were getting cold. Cold and tough.
You couldn't eat cold crumpet. Even if Jackman
were to get up and go, now this minute, it would
be too late. His afternoon was done for. Jackman had ended what Cartwright had begun.

"Your wanting God is your instinct. Trust
your instinct. You can't trust your reason.
Reason will never solve the moral problem.
Not *your* reason, nor mine, Jackman."

"It isn't my reason, it's my instincts that are
up against him."

"No, Jackman. All this trouble of yours
means that you don't *understand* God."

"I know it does, sir, still——"

"Still—what sort of God would he be if you
did understand him?"

He had him there. But Jackman raised his
head, with a gesture of defiance.

"He would at least be the kind of God who
didn't outrage my moral sense. If I can't trust
my reason I can trust my conscience."

"I'm not so sure. It's quite clear to me that
your conscience is in a very morbid state. You're
not well. You should look after your health
more carefully than I think you do. If you were

to eat fresh fruit, now, every morning before breakfast—*any* fresh fruit—you'd be a better man, and these difficulties would pass out of your mind as if they had never been."

"You think," said Mr. Jackman, with a sudden dreadful humour, "I should find God if I ate fresh fruit?"

"I think that very probably you would find God. Especially if you left off looking for him."

"You're laughing at me."

"My dear fellow, I assure you I never felt less like laughing in my life."

"You say I don't believe because I'm not well. It's the other way about. I'm not well because I can't believe. It wouldn't matter so much if I were a layman, but to be in the Church, not believing what I preach, not believing in the Sacraments I administer, not believing in my own prayers, can you imagine anything more damnable?"

The Rector couldn't. He was by this time so tired and so irritated, so irritated at not being able to show his irritation, that he couldn't imagine anything at all. He only wondered how on earth he was to appease Jackman and get him to go. He thought of him as a sort of lunatic; not dangerous, but very troublesome.

"That's my problem, sir, the simple practical problem of whether I ought to stay in the Church or to go out of it. That's what I hoped you might help me to see."

"Do you want to put the responsibility on me?"

Mr. Jackman was silent.

"I don't think it's fair of you, Jackman."

Yes. That was what it was. Unfair. It was very selfish and inconsiderate of Jackman.

"I only want your advice. I know you'll judge my case with no personal feeling. You'll see things as they are. I can only see them as I feel."

"I can't advise you."

He was not thinking of Jackman at the moment. He was thinking that it was ten minutes to five and that he was due at Mrs. Hancock's. He had a vision of Mrs. Hancock, looking charming, sitting in her little drawing-room, waiting for him. She would be waiting for him, for he had told her he would call on Thursday or Friday.

"It is surely a matter for your own conscience," he said at last.

"I can't trust my own conscience."

"You told me just now you could."

"That," said Mr. Jackman, "was in another matter."

"It was. And do you mean to tell me, Jackman, that you will trust your conscience to judge and condemn your God, when you will not trust it to decide a simple question that concerns yourself alone?"

Again he had him.

"I think it concerns you, too, sir. Do you want me to go or stay?"

The Rector weighed it. Did he want him to stay? To come again and again with his scruples and his doubts and his soul's agonies, to subject him to another ordeal like this? Did he want to become Jackman's spiritual dumping-ground? He did not. But did he want him to go? Jackman was useful. He could take funerals and week-day services. He could preach sermons. Very bad sermons, but every bad sermon Jackman preached saved the Rector from having to preach a good one. And the senior curate was punctual with his parish work. He had no fatiguing energy like Cartwright, no enthusiasm, no plans. He would never exact co-operation in some new and peace-destroying scheme. You could go away for a month's holiday and know that the parish would be as well looked after as if you were there. It would be a wretched nuisance hunting about for a substitute, and he might find himself saddled with another Cartwright.

"I don't want you to go," he said. "I think you will do well to stay. There's one cure for this trouble, and that is work. Hard work. If any man will do his will he shall know of the doctrine whether it be of God. Doing is knowing."

"You don't think, sir, I've left anything undone?"

"No. No. Your work has been excellent. The only question is whether this parish gives you enough of it."

"I hope you will give me all you can, sir."

"I will. In fact, I thought of going away for a few weeks' holiday at the end of the month." He had thought of it that minute. It was one way out of all these accumulating worries. "You'll have quite enough to do to keep things going till I come back, and perhaps by that time you'll be in another state of mind."

"I'm afraid not, sir. But I shall at least know whether I ought to go or stay."

He rose. At last he rose. He was actually going.

"Well, don't do anything hastily. But remember, the ultimate decision rests with you."

Which was as much as to say, for goodness' sake don't come worrying *me* about it again.

He looked at the clock. He had just time to get to Kempston Maisey by half past five.

CHAPTER VI

MRS. HANCOCK'S little house stood behind an iron railing at the top of the three-cornered grass-plot which was Kempston Maisey Green. A beech tree in the middle of the grass plot guarded her gate. Pale grey walls, roof of mouse-grey stone, rising and falling in low ridges and hollows; gables leaning slightly askew. A pointed porch, two convex windows on each side, five flat windows above, nine windows with small eighteenth century panes. The green door stood open. You went up a short flagged path from the gate to the threshold. The garden was at one side behind a long grey wall.

In her little drawing-room that was all black oak and blue and white china and willow pattern chintz, Mrs. Hancock waited. She sat by the side window that looked on the garden; the green lawn and yew hedges were behind her, held in the window frame. Her face, delicate and firm as if carved out of ivory, her black hair brushed straight back from her forehead and bunched out over her ears, her slender body in its light gown, rose up clear out of the green.

Canon Chamberlain stood for a moment in the doorway, looking, holding his basket of peaches. How charming she was, how young and pretty, sitting like that with the strong light behind her; he could see her black eyes shining in her delicate, slender face. Black and ivory white. He was not sorry that her husband had died in Gallipoli, and that she had had seven years to get over it in.

She rose; they came forward; they shook hands; he bowed over hers; he offered his peaches.

"Oh, how nice of you. I think you don't know my sister, Mrs. Rivers?"

He turned. They were not alone. A woman had risen from the oak settle by the hearth place; the high back of it had hidden her as he entered.

"No," she said. "You don't know me."

She was taller than Mrs. Hancock and rounder; but her face was the face of her sister; rose white skin for ivory, and gold hair and brown-gold eyes for black. Mrs. Rivers was beautiful. But he wished she was not there. Kitty Hancock ought to have told him she was not going to be alone.

"Would you think," Kitty said, "she was my sister?"

"Why not? There's a likeness, isn't there?"

"So they say." Mrs. Hancock bent over the basket. "Oh, but what beauties. You must have robbed yourself."

"No. No. The trees are bearing very well this year. I'd have been glad to rob myself if you like peaches."

"If I like them! I adore them. So does Sylvia. Don't you, Sylvia?"

But Sylvia looked apathetic; she looked sad; she looked mysterious. Yes, mysterious was the word. Her apathy and sadness annoyed him, and he hated mystery. That was not what he had come for. He had looked to this visit for a happy ending to his broken day, and Mrs. Rivers's presence was another disaster. He didn't care how beautiful she was. If only she would get up and go.

He turned to Kitty Hancock who seemed to be listening, waiting for him to say something.

"Why didn't you come for tea?" she said.

"I couldn't. Jackman called just as I was starting. He stayed an hour."

"What's the matter with Mr. Jackman?"

"The matter with him?"

"Yes. Something's the matter. He looks awful."

"Not more awful, I think, than usual."

He wasn't going to tell her what was the matter with Jackman. He never discussed his parishioners' affairs even when they had become public, and Jackman's affair was peculiarly private. So private, he considered, that it ought to have remained between Jackman and his God. He had no business to know anything about it. Kitty's curiosity must go unsatisfied.

"Is he in love?" she said. "Or what?"

"No. He isn't. And if he was I shouldn't tell you."

"You think I oughtn't to ask?"

"I think I oughtn't to answer—if I knew anything; but I don't."

"Oh, you are a nice safe person. Do you know, if I'd done something wrong, I mean something horribly wrong, the sort of thing that people keep to themselves when it's killing them, I should want to confess to you."

"You couldn't do anything horribly wrong if you tried."

"No, but *if* I did, you'd be a lovely person to tell it to. I should feel that my secret was safe, absolutely safe, buried in a tomb with a heavy slab on the top. I don't believe you'd ever even think of it again."

"Wouldn't I?" He was conscious of Mrs. Rivers listening, intensely listening.

"No. And you'd take such a nice sensible view of it. There wouldn't be any sentimental silliness about you."

He laughed. "Thank you." And she went on.

"I could trust you to tell me the whole horrid truth."

Mrs. Rivers bowed her head. He could see her brown-gold eyes looking at him from under her bent forehead. His sense of her mystery deepened unpleasantly. If *she* had a secret he didn't want to know it.

"You wouldn't be afraid of hurting me," said Kitty.

"I should be very much afraid of hurting you. I couldn't bear to hurt you."

"I wouldn't care. You'd be safe," she repeated.

"What makes you think so?"

"Because I've noticed that you never let out one little thing about anybody. You always snub people if they begin talking about each other, even if they're saying what everybody knows.

. . . I wonder if it's pure kindness, or whether
____"

"Whether?"

"Whether you simply don't care."

"You might give me the benefit of the doubt.
Would you like to confess to me if I wasn't
kind?"

"Yes. It's your kindness I should be afraid
of. If I'd done anything really wrong. Wouldn't
you, Sylvia?"

Sylvia turned her beautiful, apathetic head.

"Wouldn't I what?"

"Hate to confess to a *kind* person."

"Why?"

"Because he'd make you all weak and sloppy
when you wanted to be strong."

"I don't know," said Sylvia. "I'm not given
to confessing. And I don't know how a kind
person would make me feel." She got up. "I'm
going out. Do you want anything from the village?"

"No, dear, thank you. Don't tire yourself."

Mrs. Rivers, moving slowly in her too great
beauty, went out of the room. He was glad she
had gone.

Kitty watched her go.

"I'm worried about her," she said. "There's something the matter with *her,* if you like."

"You see," he said, "I don't ask you what it is."

"You don't care."

"I care if *you* care."

"I can't tell you what it is. I don't know myself. I wish I did. . . ."

He listened, trying hard to look as if he cared. But he wished that Mrs. Rivers hadn't left this trail of herself, this mystery, coming between him and Kitty Hancock. Kitty would be quick to see any lack of sympathy, of sincerity.

"That's what bothers me," she said. "Do you think I ought to ask her? To try and make her tell me? Or ought I to leave her to herself?"

"If she hasn't told you, perhaps she doesn't want you to know. You'd better leave her to herself."

"Sometimes—I think she *wants* to tell me."

"Well, keep your door open. That's all you can do."

It sounded well: "Keep your door open." But the real thought in his mind was "Let sleeping dogs lie." If only Sylvia would go on sleeping.

"Oh, all my doors are wide open. Sylvia knows that."

"Well then, I wouldn't force her confidence. She said she wasn't given to confessing."

"Oh, confessing. It wouldn't be anything that Sylvia had to *confess*. I expect it's something to do with Peter."

"Peter——?"

"Her husband. Colonel Rivers. He's out in Mespot, you know. That's enough to worry her, isn't it?"

"Quite enough. But you musn't let her worry *you*."

"Oh, *me*. *I* don't matter."

"You matter more than anything."

He hadn't meant to say that. His voice sounded queer and thick, not like his own voice.

He leaned back, looking at her under half-closed eyelids. She was aware of his looking.

"I oughtn't to have asked you about Mr. Jackman. It was awful of me. You thought it was awful of me, didn't you?"

"No, my dear lady, no."

"It's only because I'm sorry for the poor thing. He looks as if somebody ought to look after him."

"I assure you, Jackman is perfectly capable of looking after himself."

There was a pause. He had made an awkwardness, as if he reproved her for her interest in Jackman. He didn't like her to be interested in Jackman, so he tried to turn her interest back to himself.

"And why do you not consiaer me a kind person?" He really wanted to know why.

"But I do. It was kind of you to bring me those peaches. It's kind of you to send soup to all the sick people. It was kind of you not to talk about Jackman."

"You said you didn't know whether that was kindness or whether I didn't care."

"It sounds as if *I* wasn't a very kind person."

"Not very kind to me. But all the same adorable."

"Did I say I didn't know?"

"You did."

"Of course I know. Of course you're kind. And of course you care."

"Then what did you mean just now?"

"I suppose I meant that you'd never let your caring blind you to the truth."

"That wasn't what you *said."*

His voice was mischievous and at the same time caressing, and altogether queer.

"You musn't mind what I say."

"But I do mind. I mind very much."

"When I let my silly tongue run away with me?"

"Did it run away?"

"Yes, it did. Ever so far from the truth."

He closed his eyes. Was it to shut out the light of truth? Or not to see her? Sometimes it hurt him to see her.

"You're tired?" she said. And he opened his eyes again.

"Yes," he said, "I'm tired. I've had a heavy day."

He wanted her to pity him.

"Jackman came first thing before tea and stayed an hour talking. And Cartwright came first thing after lunch and stayed an hour talking. He was bursting with plans."

"I know. He was here at tea-time bursting."

"And before lunch I had the district visitors, Miss Lambert and Miss Wrinch, and we stayed talking for hours."

"Oh, if you've had Miss Lambert and Miss Wrinch you must be *done*."

"I am. And first thing after breakfast it was Lawson. *He* stayed an hour talking. About the War Memorial. Abused me like a pickpocket because I wouldn't put it in the market place.

"I know. And why wouldn't you?"

Slowly and with great patience he went over it yet again, giving her his reasons as he had given them to Lawson, to Miss Lambert and to Cartwright: The sanctity of the War Memorial; the Church's righteous claim; his welcome to the Nonconformists.

Kitty looked tender and sad. She didn't respond as Miss Lambert had responded. She seemed to be keeping back her thoughts.

"You don't agree with me?" he said and realised how more than anything it was *her* agreement that he wanted.

"I'm sorry. But I'm afraid I don't. It is rather hiding it away from the poor things. It's *their* Memorial. It's *their* sons and brothers and husbands and sweethearts. And it's awful that the Nonconformists should have to go sneaking in, being let in, as if they hadn't the right——"

"I'm sorry. I felt sure that you would see it as I see it."

"I do see it as you see it. But I see it as they see it too. And it's they who matter. I don't say it because my husband's name's on the Memorial."

It was. He had forgotten it. Forgotten Kitty's husband who had died in Gallipoli.

"I don't care whether Gerald's name stands in

the church or in the market place. It's glorious anyway. I do care that all those dear people shouldn't be hurt. And I don't want *you* to be hurt either by giving them the chance to say cruel things about you. Mr. Cartwright and I were talking about it. He agrees with me."

"You mean you agree with him?" He said it with a little spurt of jealousy.

"No. He agrees with me. I mean about you; that it's not fair to you."

"Ah, my dear lady, if *you're* fair to me, I don't care what they say."

"Fair to you? Of course I'm fair. Why shouldn't I be?"

Her coolness checked him.

"Do you see much of Cartwright?" He said it as casually as if the question had no importance.

"Oh, yes. He runs in and out. He plays with my children. He's devoted to children. And they're devoted to him."

He felt a cold shivering at his heart.

"You know," he said. "I've hardly seen your children. They're never here when I come."

"I don't let them be. I don't want them to bore you."

"Would they bore me?"

"They'a worry the life out of you. They're dreadfully rampageous."

"If Cartwright can stand them I should think I might."

He thought that would pass for sincerity, but he was not sincere. He couldn't stand even the thought of Kitty's children. And on several occasions he had heard sounds that terrified him.

"Mr. Cartwright's different," she said. "He's nothing but a big child himself."

At that moment a whoop and a scream went up from the garden. Five children had rushed from somewhere unknown and had broken loose on the lawn. He could see two tall and slender boys, two girls and a little boy.

"They're not all yours?" he said. He had thought there were three of them.

"Yes, all mine."

Five. Not three. Five.

"Not—those big boys?" he said. "They're not *your* sons?"

"Yes. They're my eldest. They're tall for their ages. Wilfrid's only fifteen."

"It's odd," he said. "I hadn't realised them."

"Well, then," she answered, "you'll realise them now. They're making noise enough."

The cold gathered about his heart.

"Shall we go out and look at them?" she said. "They've got some tremendous game on."

Did he wish, really wish, to be nearer to that game? The boys whooped and the girls screamed. A round, dangerous body as large as a cannon ball, rushed through the air. A croquet mallet followed it.

Oh, that awful chill at his heart. He was seized with a doubt of his own wisdom, and that doubt was ghastly. He wondered whether he had gone too far. He had been saying things to Kitty Hancock. What things? He remembered. He could hear himself saying them, and his voice seemed to him to have fairly throbbed with meaning: "You matter more than anything. . . . I do mind. I mind very much. . . . If you're fair to me I don't care what they say." He had said she was adorable. What interpretation would she put on that? Surely, surely, he had not committed himself to anything more than friendly admiration?

She led him down a long passage. The two big boys were taking more croquet balls and more mallets from the cloak-room at the end. Wilfrid and Bertie. Wilfrid was fifteen; Bertie thirteen. They were slender, ivory white and black like their mother. They looked at him with wild, innocent faces, a little distrustful and defiant. But they bore the introduction with every appearance of good breeding; they were not Kitty's sons for nothing.

It was the noise they made afterwards that decided him, that turned his doubt, his ghastly doubt, into a strong, wise certainty. He would go no further.

It seemed that whooping and screaming were part of the game they had on. It was not croquet, for the great thing about it was that no ball and no child stood still for a second. It was like no game on earth that he had ever seen; a game of perpetual motion, of perpetual noise and violence, all five children playing at once. The posts were goals. There were no hoops. Mallets swang in the air like golf sticks. Balls were sent flying at a terrific pace in all directions, hitting each other or missing. The children raced up and down the lawn, at top speed, pursuing their balls. The hit ball passed to the hitter, and round it there raged a game like hockey, with more whooping and screaming. It seemed to him that Mrs. Hancock encouraged them to whoop and scream. The more noise they made the better she liked it.

She turned to him, "What do you think of it?"
It's a great game, isn't it?"

She began to explain the game. "Wilfrid invented it. It's called Cruggerhock, because it combines all the merits of croquet, hockey, cricket and rugger."

"Perhaps it does. I can't imagine a more noisy, violent and dangerous game."

"The beauty of it is that everybody can play at it at once. You should see Mr. Cartwright play it."

"He would. It would give scope for his boisterous energy."

She wasn't really thinking about Cartwright. Her eyes were fixed on her children.

"They're dear things," she said. "You *do* realise them, don't you?"

He smiled a little wryly.

Oh yes, he realised them.

"Because, if you don't, you won't realise me."

"Won't I?"

Oh, she was honest. It was as if she had said "You see what you'd have been let in for if you'd gone further. But I didn't mean you to go." As if she had said, "The way to me lies through my children, but you'll never take it."

That was why she had brought him out to look

at them, why she encouraged them to whoop and scream, that he might know the worst and draw back in time.

"Oh, look at Timmy—my baby—how he gave that great swipe."

He looked at the little black and ivory boy, Kitty's seven year old baby, and tried to smile again.

"Some mothers," she said, "are minxes. They like their boys best. I hope *I* don't. Aren't Betty and Jenny darlings?"

"Weren't you just like them at their age?"

"Yes, I was. I was much, much nicer then than I am now."

"You don't expect me to agree with you?"

"No, I don't, because you don't care for children."

"Oh, come," he said.

"You don't, really. You hate their awful noises. If you stayed a week with them you'd be miserable. You couldn't bear to be shut up for ten minutes alone with one of them. And even that would be better than all of them together."

How well she knew him.

He laughed, but he didn't lie to her. She would have seen through any lie.

"Even I find them a bit wearisome sometimes. And they matter more to me than anything on earth."

"I know they do." He said it with a certain emotion.

"Well, you've had enough of them, you shan't be bored any more. Shall we go in?"

"I'm afraid," he said, "I must be going."

"Oh, must you? I'll tell them to be quiet if you'll stay."

"No. I won't make them hate me. That reminds me, I've got to look in at the Girls' Club this evening."

"I *am* sorry for you. You don't mean to say you let Hilda rope you in?"

"I did indeed."

"Well, it'll be awful. Worse than Cruggerhock."

It would. It would be horribly hot. Somebody would thump out a frightful tune on a cracked piano, and they would dance, they would turn round and round, imperfectly washed, horribly hot; they would stamp on the uneven floor, beating up clouds of poisonous dust that would injure his throat.

"The rector of the parish can't call his soul his own."

"Well," she said. "I'll pray for it. Poor soul. Good-bye, if you won't stay."

She went with him through the house to the gate in the garden railings. There was a yell from the garden. She smiled. Her face as they parted was happy and serene, yet with a certain tenderness and pity. She was sorry for him; she had called him "Poor soul."

He drove in his governess cart, along the quiet, grey-white road, past farm and spinney, cornfield and pasture, down Drayton Street, past the slums of Queningford, over the stone bridge above the Colne and through the market place, past the old Green Dragon and the King's Head and up the Rectory drive to his grey, calm-fronted house.

He sat in his drawing-room, waiting for his dinner. He had a vision of Kitty's five children chasing each other through his drawing-room, among the fragile, valuable furniture; or trampling down his well-ordered, perfect garden, in the frenzy of Cruggerhock; ravaging his fruit trees. Their yells sounded through the quiet house. He saw their defiant, distrustful faces; Kitty's children; they hated him because he loved peace. And he felt the blessedness of deliverance. He had been on the edge of an incredible folly. Kitty had seen him hovering; she had taken him by the hand and shown him his danger and led him very gently away. Kitty had saved him. Therefore he thought very tenderly and gratefully of Kitty. Kind, wise, and honourable Kitty.

Another sort of woman might have made it very unpleasant for him, for he had gone further than he had meant to go.

The Girls' Club was even more horrible than Cruggerhock; it smelt worse. All boisterous energy, smell and dust it was. Never again would he let himself be drawn in. Never again.

CHAPTER VII

THAT was on a Friday. The next morning he shut himself up in his study and prepared his sermon for Sunday evening. It was especially addressed to Jackman and the district visitors, for their inspiration and encouragement.

He had taken for his text John, ix. 4, "I must work the works of him that sent me while it is day."

"I am going to speak to you this evening about Work: the beauty of Work: the rightness, holiness and blessedness of Work. Some of you will perhaps say that Work can be a curse as well as a blessing; they will point to the hard, grinding toil that brutalizes men and women, to the dangerous trades, to labour under foul, insanitary conditions such as still exist in some of our big cities, labour that is sheer, soulless slavery. Well, I am not upholding slavery, I am not saying that Work under insanitary conditions is a holy and a blessed thing; but I do say that the evils of sloth are even greater, more degrading, more brutalizing than our worst industries. And if I had to choose between utter idleness and the hardest of hard labour, it is not idleness that I should choose. For idleness saps the will, undermines our whole moral nature; it strikes at the root of all that is spiritual in us. It is the parent of all the vices. Of drinking, drugging, and worse; of all the evil habits that debase humanity. The idle man is potentially, if not actually, a vicious man."

He wished he could have made the point that idleness was the parent of murder, there had been so many murders lately, but when he came to think of it most of them had been committed by members of the working or professional classes. He went on, his pen running fluently and his mind checking it; for he desired to be truthful.

"The social evil is due——"

Was it? Working men and professional men also—— Well then, better say, "in great measure."

"The social evil is due in great measure to idleness——"

Yet stay. Prostitutes were idle.

"It is maintained entirely by an idle class, a class that has refused——"

No, this was not always the case. He must be just.

"A class that has either refused, or, to our shame, been denied all honest means of livelihood.

"The general unrest and trouble of our time is due to enforced idleness, to the existence in our midst of an immense body of the unemployed. What is the greatest national catastrophe next to war or revolution? A general strike. What is the worst consequence of anarchy? The dislocation of industry.

"There was once a great painter——"

Was Madox Brown a great painter? Perhaps not. But it would sound better if he said he was.

"A great painter who in one of his walks happened to see a group of labourers making a road. He made a picture of what he saw; the men in their corduroys and shirt sleeves, the bare arms wielding picks and spades and mallets."

Mallets. His mind wandered, and he thought of Mrs. Hancock's children and their dreadful play. They *were* mallets, those huge wooden hammers workmen used for driving stakes in. If there were no mallets in Madox Brown's picture there ought to have been.

"He called that picture *Work*. He painted it to show the beauty and dignity of Work. I wish that a copy of that picture could hang in every home."

But he didn't want one in his own drawing-room.

"Nowhere in the Sacred Books of any of the great religions is there more praise of Work than in our own Bible."

He was not absolutely sure of this; but he judged it a safe guess; the Jews were notoriously an industrial people.

"In the New Testament alone we have the sayings of our Lord: I must work the works of him that sent me while it is day. My Father worketh hitherto and I work. If I do not the work of my Father believe me not; but if I do, though ye believe not me, believe the works. Herein is my Father glorified that ye bear much fruit. We have the parable of the talents and the vineyard. We have the testimony of St. Paul: Not slothful in business: fervent in spirit: serving the Lord. Bear ye one another's burdens. Be not weary in well-doing. With good will doing service. Work out your own salvation with fear and trembling. Being fruitful in every good work."

This was becoming monotonous. He must leave St. Paul.

"The author of the Epistle to the Hebrews says: Make you perfect in every good work to do His will. And we have St. James. Be ye doers of the word and not hearers only. I could multiply texts."

If he got on to St. James he would never have done.

"In Genesis we have the great seven days' Work of creation. To be sure we read that God rested on the seventh day; but we should not understand this as a final cessation of his Work. He created no more worlds. But he had still to maintain the worlds that he had created. When you remember that we and all the animals are dependent on God for every breath we draw, that not only the earth and the other stars but every atom in this vast universe is dependent on him for its perpetual movement, we may imagine how tremendous and how unceasing is the Work of God that keeps the universe going. God's rest is only

'Central peace subsisting at the heart
Of boundless agitation' . . . "

Ought he to let it stand? Wasn't the flight just a little bit over the heads of his congrega-

tion? N-no. On the whole he thought he would
keep it. An obscure passage in a sermon chal-
lenged attention. People wondered what you
meant by it. They talked it over; and that sermon was remembered when many a clearer one
was forgotten.

"True, there remaineth a rest for the people
of God; but we are told to labour therefore to
enter into that rest. Let us resist the very first
approaches of this sin of sloth. Let us discipline ourselves, if it is only by rising half an hour
earlier every morning; by going out when we
wish to sit comfortably indoors; by shaking off
that insidious drowsiness that comes over us
sometimes in the afternoon; by performing punctually some unpleasant task.

"Never lose sight of the rightness, the holiness, the blessedness of Work. Of all honest
Work, whether it be the Work of the thinker, of
the poet, the musician, the painter; the Work of
the teacher; the skilled Work of the artisan; the
humble Work of the farm labourer. To scrub
a floor, to cook a meal well——"

(He thought of Fuller.)

"—is beautiful and honourable. In all these
worketh that one and the self-same Spirit, divid-
ing to every man severally as he will.

√ "Work is not only good for the body, it is the cure for every mental and spiritual ill. Are you worried? Work. Are you hopeless and depressed? Work. Are you troubled with religious doubts——"

He thought of Jackman.

"Work harder than ever. If any man will do his will he shall know of the doctrine whether it be of God. Doing is knowing.

"During the Great War everybody was busy. Many of us found in Work an aim and object that had been missing hitherto. Strange to say, under that awful calamity they were happier than they had ever been before. And this shows that no evil is absolute. God's power was manifested in bringing good out of the most horrible catastrophe that has been known in history."

That would be one for Jackman, with his either impotent or immoral God.

"Perhaps some of us have become slack again in this time of peace. Perhaps some of you will ask What Work is there for me to do here in Queningford? Well, I say there is plenty of Work: there are the Sunday schools; the Mother's Meetings; there are sick and old people to be visited and people in trouble; there are clothes to be made for the poor; food to be taken to them.

Nobody need be idle. If there is nothing to be done, there are always things to be thought of, words that may be said."

His mind was wandering again. He wanted to stop writing his sermon and get back to *Madame Bovary*. There was that long article on Economics in the *Nineteenth Century* that he had still to tackle. But he knew he wasn't going to tackle it, just yet. As long as there was a good novel within reach, he was haunted like a child with a box of chocolates, he couldn't keep his hands off it till the last sweet was eaten.

He pulled himself together and worked up to his close.

"For even worse than laziness of body is laziness of the mind and heart. Laziness of the mind: the refusal to consider some unfamiliar aspect of the truth, to grapple with some question of national importance, because of the slight mental effort involved. Laziness of the heart: lack of sympathy, inattention, failure to respond; unreadiness to enter into another person's state of mind, to listen to the tale of his joys and sorrows, his hopes and fears, because they may not greatly interest us."

He thought of Jackman. *He* had listened to Jackman.

"The good life is that in which every day some problem has been solved, some practical difficulty faced and overcome; some kind deed done, if it is only the patient listening to a friend's dull story. Let us guard aaginst that sin of sloth, of the deaf ear, the unseeing eye, the unheeding and unremembering mind.

"Believe me, there is but a step between such a state and that worst of all states—apathy of soul: when we can no longer feel deeply, think clearly, and will with decision, when we are dead alike to the calls of conscience and to the meaning and loveliness of life."

He would end on that note. He couldn't better it.

"We must work while it is day; for the night cometh, when no man can work."

He laid down his pen. He rose, lifted up the green curtain, and with a thick sigh of content, sad down again to *Madame Bovary*.

CHAPTER VIII

THE Rector was perfectly serious about his holiday. It was a great inspiration which he owed to Jackman. But for the annoyance caused by Jackman and his doubts he would not have thought of leaving Queningford this year. But it would be a good thing to get away from Queningford for a while, to get away from Cartwright and Jackman and Miss Wrinch, to get clean away from Mrs. Hancock. To have nothing, absolutely nothing to do for the next three weeks and nobody to interfere with his doing it.

He went down to South Cornwall. He stayed at the best hotel in the place and spent his days lying out on a long chair in the garden, sitting on the cliffs, strolling down to the little town to change his novels at the circulating library, smoking and reading the papers in the lounge, talking to the Colonel (between them they left the Government without a shred on its back), playing bridge, and avoiding the other clergyman whom he believed to be tainted with evangelicalism. Or he looked on while the Colonel's pretty wife wound her silk into balls and knitted it into jumpers. He had an air of being initiated into the mysteries, hypnotised by the white, twinkling hands. The Colonel's wife reminded him of Mrs. Hancock.

He talked to her about the Riviera (she had been there); about Cannes and Antibes and Villefranche and Nice; about eucalyptus trees and the soft, powdery smell of mimosa; about the food at the Californie Hotel. It would never be the same again since the war, he said; and she said No, it would never be the same. Simple, easy, well-bred conversations, flowing on, with long tranquil silences between.

Nobody annoyed him. Nobody talked to him about parish work and religious doubts. Nobody asked his advice. Nobody disagreed with him. Nothing, except the occasional appearance of the other clergyman, broke in upon his peace. He hadn't got to listen to anybody unless he wanted to. The links were some little way off, and the tennis courts couldn't be seen from the garden where he sat; so that he was not disturbed by the sight of people taking violent and unnecessary exercise. The Colonel, his companion, was as innocent of all activity as himself.

Peaches, packed in cotton wool, were sent down to him from Queningford. He kept them in his bedroom to eat every morning before breakfast. Sometimes he offered one to the Colonel's pretty wife who reminded him of Mrs. Hancock.

Altogether it was a very happy time. The food at the hotel was good and the beds comfortable, yet not so good and comfortable but that he was glad to get back to the Rectory and Fuller.

That was in September.

He hadn't been back twenty-four hours before Cartwright—*Cartwright*—called. About the Services for Men Only. The Rector had said that he would let him know whether he might hold them.

Now the Rector regarded those services as the thin end of an awful wedge that must before long heave him up out of his state of bliss. There was enough to do on Sunday in all conscience, without four-o'clock services. Tea-time too.

"No, Cartwright, I can't have it. I've been thinking it over." He hadn't. Mercifully he had forgotten the four-o'clock services while he was away. "And it won't do."

"Why not, sir?"

"Because that kind of thing isn't suitable for a

country parish. It's all very well in a big town where you get all the vices."

"We've got them here, sir, I assure you."

"Not to any extent that would justify you. Our people have their faults, but the public vice you mean isn't among them."

"Don't you know, sir, that there's a whole gang of prostitutes in the alleys off Drayton Street? Places where the district visitors don't go. There's a girl, Polly Tombs, who dances on a table every night at the Three Magpies. That's the kind of thing we've got to contend with. I don't believe it would happen if the lads knew what they were doing; if somebody they respected had the courage to get up and tell them straight. They go about it in a half-hearted, furtive way; they think nobody knows and nobody cares. I want to show them that *we* know and *we* care."

His "we" was ominous. The Rector recognised it as the swelling of that wave which, if he were not careful, would presently engulf him.

"Anyhow," he said, "it won't do in Kempston."

"Yes, even in Kempston."

"You were talking about Queningford."

"Yes, sir; because I hoped that you will do for Queningford what I do for Kempston."

"No, Cartwright, no. I won't have it. For one you save you may corrupt a dozen. You'll be simply pandering to a morbid curiosity. That's all the good you'll do."

"I'm sorry you're not with me, sir. I'd set my heart on this."

He had now the strange, disconcerting spectacle of a downcast Cartwright. He felt sorry for Cartwright, he was so well-meaning, and he hated feeling sorry, hated that little painful tug at his heart. Cartwright had no business to make him feel like that.

"You're on the wrong tack, my dear fellow, the wrong tack," he said.

"Well, I suppose I must concentrate on my Club for all I'm worth."

"I suppose you must."

"Do you think, sir, we could raise subscriptions for the Club reading-room?"

The Rector stared in dismay.

"Do I think *I* could raise subscriptions? No, I do not."

"Can't we get up a penny reading or a concert or something?"

There was no end to Cartwright's devastating activity.

"Or a jumble sale?"

"A jumble sale, *perhaps*. You must talk to Miss Lambert about it, not to me."

"That's a good idea, sir, and we'll keep the concert for the billiard table."

"What billiard table?"

"For the Queningford Men's Club, when we've got it."

"Ah—*when*. I've told you I don't see my way yet."

"If you don't see your way to the Men's Club, don't you think we might start the evening classes in Queningford? It would make a nucleus for the Club later on."

There was no escaping the fellow; if you got loose from him in one direction he caught you in another. And he was plausible. The Rector couldn't think of any reasonable objection to the evening classes except that he shrank from the exertion of getting them up. It meant interviewing people and overcoming their very natural unwillingness to help. It wasn't enough to give out in church that classes would be held in the schoolroom at such and such an hour in the evening. If the scheme were to succeed it meant a house-to-house visiting of the lads themselves, a going out into the highways and hedges and compelling them to come in. In all this he would have to be the moving spirit, and never in its life had his spirit felt more disinclined to move.

For the Rector did not believe seriously in his lack of influence. He believed and had every reason for believing that he was the most influential person in the parish. His very inertia helped him to be all things, if not to all men, at least to all the county people. He liked visiting their rich, comfortable houses better than he liked visiting the houses of the poor. He had power over the kind of people who gave large subscriptions. His lavish hospitality and his charities made him a customer whom the tradespeople of Queningford couldn't afford to offend. He could wring subscriptions from grocers and fishmongers and stationers; and the drapers, not to be behindhand, followed suit. And he had a considerable balance at the local bank. An inertia, equal to his own, kept the whole town in an attitude of placid submission to the clergy. Lawson, the radical and infidel, and his friends the Caldecotts were exceptions and not popular themselves. The War Memorial was not going to be an everlasting stumblingblock; for in the world he moved in Nonconformists didn't count.

So in common honesty he could not go on pleading his unpopularity as his excuse.

And if he resisted Cartwright today he would be no better off. Cartwright would return again and again to the attack. He wouldn't rest till he had forced him to start evening classes in Queningford, and a Men's Club, and a fife and drum band.

He could hear it playing in Queningford market place, outside the Rectory.

No. That must never be. He must put his foot down once and forever on Cartwright's fife and drum band. After all, without him Cartwright could do nothing, except go on like the kind of nuisance that he was.

He had one argument left. His old one.

"Evening classes may be very important, but, after all, they are entirely secular. The townspeople might see to that side. I don't think that the Church is bound to take them up."

Mr. Cartwright fairly detonated.

"Forgive me, but I do, sir. I feel very strongly that taking over what you call the secular side is the Church's one chance for survival. The people will be reconciled to the Church only if they see that the Church is identified with the common life and the common interests. We churchmen can only justify our existence through direct, personal service. Personal service and the increasing secularization of the Church's outlook. Those are the great things."

As if he had never seen it before he saw now how dangerous Cartwright was. He was a young man not only with practical schemes, but with ideas. He had something like a philosophy of the priestly life. And more than practical schemes Canon Chamberlain abhorred and feared philosophy and ideas.

And that thought which had once passed through his mind came back to him and took shape.

If Cartwright went. If he could find him another curacy. A town curacy where he would have scope for his ideas, space for his energy to explode in.

Of course he might wait till Cartwright's activity had exhausted itself. At the pace he was going he would soon have nothing left to do. But no. You could set no limits to young Cartwright's activity and ingenuity. When he had done everything conceivable, he would think of something you couldn't have conceived. So long as he was in the parish he would be a cause of worry and anxiety. You would never know what he would be up to next. What was more, he would be a perpetual reproach; he would come and go, leaving a sting behind him in your conscience.

Would Cartwright consent to exchange his curacy for another? He would sound him, and see. He would make the prospect tempting.

"Cartwright," he said, "your energy amazes me, it always has amazed me. You know you're thrown away here in a small country village. You haven't got elbow room. It seems to me that you would do much better in a big town. Something more important than Kempston-Maisey."

Cartwright replied amazingly.

"No, sir. There isn't anything more important than Kempston-Maisey, unless it's Queningford. The village is *the* important factor in the social life of today. The village is the unit. It's the nursery of the larger centres; the place where everything begins. Every day, all over England, the villages are sending their young men and their young women into the big towns. That's where the fresh blood of the towns starts. Now, isn't it *the* important thing that the fresh blood we send out should be really fresh blood, pure blood? The education of the village is *the* important thing. It means that the life of the big towns depends on what we send into them. If we can send out, continually, strong, pure lads and girls, with well-trained minds and bodies, and send enough of them, we might in time regenerate the big towns. But a taint here in the village is a taint at the very source.

I wouldn't like to give up my work in Kempston."

"Yes. But almost anybody could take it up where you've begun it. I should see, personally, that it was taken up. Meanwhile I feel that your great powers and energies are being wasted here. The work is too easy for you."

That was how he could appeal to him, through that heroic longing of young Cartwright for the highest and the hardest thing; for the battle and the march, the danger and the long, difficult advance.

"You said yourself you'd set your heart on those Men's Services. Well, those Services are quite unsuitable here. But they are badly needed in the big towns. There you'd have your work cut out for you. I feel that I've no right to keep you here, seeing what you are. . . . If an opportunity arose, now, you wouldn't refuse it?"

"I should think twice before I accepted it."

"Well, think twice. Think as many times as you like."

"I see no opportunity, sir."

"You don't know what may turn up. But you do know that you would have my very warmest recommendation."

They shook hands on that and the young man left him.

CHAPTER IX

THE next day he had returned from visiting a case of sickness reported by Miss Lambert when he found Mr. Jackman waiting for him in his study. This was not exactly what he wanted after visiting a case of sickness, but he remembered that he did not yet know whether Jackman meant to go or stay, and that sooner or later he would have to see him and find out.

At the first sight of him he judged that Jackman had come to his senses and was going to stay; for, instead of showing all crushed and huddled in his attitude of dejection, the senior curate held himself upright with an air of braced and cheerful resolution.

He ordered tea and observed with satisfaction that this time Jackman ate and drank like any normal person. While the meal lasted he entertained him with an account of his holiday in the Cornish Riviera.

"They've no business to call it that," he said;

it's not to be compared for a moment with the real Riviera."

And Mr. Jackson who had not seen the real Riviera and probably never would see it, supposed that it was not. Not for a moment.

Tea over, Canon Chamberlain fixed Mr. Jackman with what he meant for a benevolent yet searching gaze.

"I'm glad," he said, "to see you looking so much better. You've come to yourself again."

"Yes, I've come to myself again."

"And have you come to—er—any final decision?"

"I have. I see my way very clearly at last."

"As I thought you would. I knew you would."

"I'm afraid, sir, it isn't at all as you thought."

"You mean—you're not thinking of leaving the Church, are you?"

"Yes, I am."

"You are still in the same unhappy state of mind?"

"Still in the same state; but not unhappy."

"Do I understand that you are no longer troubled with doubts? If so, why leave us?"

"I've more doubts than ever, sir; but they don't trouble me any more. What worried me was staying in the Church when I didn't believe

what I had to preach. Now that I'm going out
of the Church everything seems clear and easy
to me."

"But what are you going to do, Jackman?"
Let's look at the practical side of it. You've got
to live. How are you going to do it? The
Church is the profession you've been brought up
to and you're not fit for any other."

"I've thought of that. And, so far as the work
of the Church is social service, I shall not be
giving it up. I shall only be working outside the
Church instead of in it; and working harder."

"You have some definite plan in view?"

"Yes, sir. I'm going to join the Poplar Lay
Mission."

"The Poplar—Lay—Mission." He rolled it
on his tongue as if it was some luscious absurd-
ity. "And what will that entail?"

"It will entail nothing beyond willingness and
ability to work and a certain obedience to my su-
periors. What you call my state of mind won't
matter to the Mission. I shan't have to believe
in God."

"Has the Mission no religion then?"

"Not what you would call religion. It has no
creed beyond belief in love and man's duty to
man. Its work is entirely social and secular."

"That's to say, your Mission has no mission."

Mr. Jackman raised his head.

"It has a very great mission. Its mission is to feed and clothe the poor. To nurse them when they're ill. To carry on their education where the State leaves it off. To give them wholesome amusement. To reclaim drunkards, prostitutes and young criminals. To fight every form of moral and physical evil. To go to the outcasts of society and bring them back into it by showing them the love of man for man."

"A wonderful programme, Jackman. But without God it sounds to me like the play of Hamlet without Hamlet."

With Jackman he affected a tone of light banter, to show that he didn't take him seriously. He had not yet measured the awful seriousness of Jackman.

"But it isn't altogether without God. At least for me."

"How? If you refuse to believe in him——"

"I only refuse to believe in him as a past and present fact. I do believe in him as a future event."

"What on earth do you mean?"

"I mean what I say. I believe in God, not as the ultimate reality here and now, but as the ulti-

mate event. As That which is to be. This belief
has come to me instead of the faith I've lost. It
came after I'd gone down to the Mission and
seen what they're doing there."

"You went?"

"Yes, sir. I took a day off and went. The
Settlement is in the middle, of the worst slums in
Poplar. I saw it for myself; I saw the heads of
the Settlement and they told me what had been
done already in three years. I saw men and
women living and working there in surroundings
that are enough to make you sick with despair,
I found them with their minds fixed on the future, believing, hoping in the future, and it came
to me that if God doesn't exist here and now he
will exist some day. . . . When the whole work
is done and we've cleared away everything that
stands between humanity and its future. . . .
The world's full of horrors. We've got to fight
them all our lives, generation after generation,
till there are no more horrors. After all, it's the
way of evolution. *Our* struggle for existence is
the struggle against the beastliness of the beast
we came from and of the beast-man. My idea
is that, as we've evolved from the ape, so God
will be evolved from us as we rise upwards."

He twitched with excitement.

"How on earth is your God going to exist in the future if he doesn't exist here and now?"

"How do we exist here and now when we didn't exist in the past? Who could have foreseen man in the ape?"

"The possibility of him was there."

"Well then, the possibility of God is here. May I tell you what I think about it, sir?"

The Rector, stretched out at ease in his chair, made a bland gesture of permission, and Mr. Jackman, very upright and eager, went on explaining his theory of God.

"The mistake we've made has been in supposing that God exists already, that he is our Father. Our belief in the fatherhood of God has made us abjectedly dependent on him; abjectedly dependent on something not ourselves that doesn't exist. To me the abominable state of this world makes it clear that he doesn't exist; makes it blasphemy to suppose that he exists. I'm not going into all that again. He doesn't exist. At the same time, the longing for God, the need of God, is so obstinately fixed in the human heart that we can't ignore it."

"We certainly cannot."

"Well, this deep primitive instinct has evolved into the conception of God as all powerful, all wise and all good. A conception that we cannot reconcile with reality. It's nothing but our conception, our aspiration, our ideal. But it carries with it the secret of its own fulfilment. Such an ideal, from its very nature, is bound to be realised in time. It's not the beginning, it's the end, the end to which creation moves. If God hasn't created us, we must create God."

"Out of nothing?"

"Out of ourselves. He is hidden in us as the germ is hidden in the womb. The world's pain is the pain of labour, of bringing forth God. You see, we've got to change the Christian idea of God-made man to the idea of man-made God. God is not the great I AM. He is the great I SHALL BE."

"You really believe that, Jackman?"

"I really believe that. If I didn't I couldn't go through with my work in the Mission. I shall have to live and die in a filthy slum, among drunkards and prostitutes and thieves. If I hadn't that hope of deity, if I thought that humanity would always be what it is, how could I bear it?"

"I don't see how you're going to bear it as it is."

"I'm not afraid of poverty."

114

"Poverty? Is your work purely voluntary?"

"Purely. Except that the Settlement will give me lodging, light and fire. I must pay a small sum weekly for my board."

"Out of what?"

"My father will make me the same small allowance he does now. I may even be able to save a little out of it for my poor. My clothes would have been a difficulty, but a cousin has promised me his old suits."

"Well, Jackman, I don't know what to say."

He didn't. It made him feel horribly uncomfortable to think of Jackman living in a filthy slum, and starving himself to feed his poor, and wearing his cousin's old suits. Jackman had never given him such an intolerable half-hour. At the same time he felt that he could not pass over Jackman's awful blasphemy without rebuke.

"But I shouldn't be doing my duty if I didn't tell you that your belief, if it is your belief, is rank blasphemy. Nonsensical blasphemy. I've never heard anything so ridiculous from any human being. I may tell you that if you had wished to stay with me I couldn't have kept you holding the views you do. If I can call them views. There isn't any reason in them or shadow of reason."

"You said I wasn't to trust my reason, sir."

"Well, I shouldn't if I were you."

"I don't. I trust my instincts. I'm sorry if I've said anything distasteful to you."

"Distasteful is hardly the right word. Abominable."

"I'm sorry. I shall ask you to judge me by my work. If I give a good account of myself at Poplar, perhaps you'll forgive me."

"I do forgive you, Jackman."

"And when you judge me will you remember that in all this misery, at my very worst, I never lost for one minute my love for man nor my faith in man."

"What is that, my dear boy, without love for God and faith in God?"

"Why," said Mr. Jackman, "I've been trying to show you that it's the same thing."

"It isn't. That's your grand mistake. But I hope that everything will be well with you, and that your charity will bring back your faith."

He held out his hand. He smiled his most benignant smile. He went with Mr. Jackman to the front door and saw him go. He didn't feel entirely safe till the iron gates of the drive had clanged on his retreat.

He was glad that Jackman was going. He was

the most uncomfortable person he had ever met. Worse, far worse than Cartwright. Cartwright only interfered with his body's peace; Jackman, if he had let him, would have utterly destroyed his peace of mind.

CHAPTER X

WITH Jackman gone, and Cartwright removed to another curacy, his peace would be perfect. The trouble was to find a suitable substitute for Cartwright. He must have an older man, forty-five, at the very least, a man without too many ideas in his head, who wouldn't worry him with perpetual experiments, yet a man with sufficient experience of routine work to be trusted in Kempston by himself.

So that it seemed positively Providential when his old friend, Wildon Fawcett, of St. Simon and St. Jude's Church, Bristol, wrote to him to ask if he knew of anybody who would be glad to exchange a country curacy for his. The work of St. Simon and St. Jude's was increasing beyond Mr. Fawcett's and his wife's power to cope with it, and they desired to remove themselves to some country parish where life was less acutely strenuous. St. Simon and St. Jude's, he said, was a splendid opening for a young man with energy and initiative. If he was interested in social reform so much the better; he would have an unlimited field for his activity. Mr. Fawcett said St. Simon and St. Jude's was in great and crying need of that help which only a younger and more energetic man than he could give. The present incumbent of St. Simon and St. Jude's was a seventy-year-old invalid who left everything to his curate. The curate was practically Vicar and could do what he liked in St. Simon and St. Jude's without fear of obstruction.

It was the very thing for Cartwright. And Wildon Fawcett as he remembered him, docile and devoted, hardworking in his groove, innocent of ideas, destitute of all the qualities that had annoyed him in Cartwright, Wildon Fawcett was the very man for Kempston Maisey. He would settle down there in perfect peace, undisturbed and undisturbing. And he had a wife who would help in the parish work.

He wrote to Fawcett and said that he thought he had the very curacy for him here in his own parish, and that his present junior curate would be the very man for St. Simon and St. Jude's; if they could agree on the exchange.

And he wrote to his present junior curate and said that the curacy of St. Simon and St. Jude's,

Bristol, was the very thing for Cartwright. He would be practically Vicar there, which, the Rector felt, was what he ought to be. Queningford parish wasn't big enough to hold two rectors, and Mr. Cartwright's administrative powers were thrown away in it. And he thought that after their recent conversation Mr. Cartwright would be prepared for the change. Sorry as he would be to lose him, he urged him very earnestly to make it; for his own sake as entering on a larger sphere of usefulness, and for the sake of St. Simon and St. Jude's as a Macedonia which was fairly crying out for Cartwright to come over and help it. It was, he said, purely Providential; for he had had no idea of Mr. Fawcett's plans when he spoke to Cartwright.

And Cartwright came rushing over on his bicycle, to say that it all depended on Mr. Fawcett. If Mr. Fawcett was prepared to carry out his plans for Kempston Maisey, he was prepared to relieve Mr. Fawcett of his curacy of St. Simon and St. Jude's. But he couldn't go if he felt that his work in Kempston Maisey would be undone or left unfinished.

And Canon Chamberlain replied that he could trust Mr. Fawcett who was known personally and intimately to himself. Mr. Fawcett had had

a long and hard experience of parish work, and
Mr. Cartwright might rest assured that his plans
for Kempston Maisey would be in good hands.
And were we not, all of us, too apt to think ourselves indispensable?

"Can I see him, sir; and tell him what's been
done and what we meant to do?"

"Certainly, Cartwright. The best thing would
be for Mr. Fawcett to come over for the week-
end and for you to meet him here."

And so Mr. Fawcett got somebody else to take
his Services for him and came over to Queningford the day before the Harvest Festival. It
was arranged that he and Canon Chamberlain
should lunch at the Manor on Sunday morning
and go to tea with Mrs. Hancock in the afternoon, and that Mr. Fawcett should preach in
Kempston Church in the evening, Mr. Cartwright taking the Service for Canon Chamberlain at Queningford.

Mr. Fawcett arrived just before tea-time on
Saturday afternoon. He presented the same innocent and lovable appearance that Canon Chamberlain remembered: the same slender, sloping
figure, the same pink flush, the same features all
in peaceable retreat, all but the rosy bulb of the
lower lip which stuck out between the fair wisp

of moustache and the straggling, retreating beard. The same gentle, blue, shortsighted eyes looked out at him from behind the big round glasses. He approached the Rector with extreme gentleness, beside him young Cartwright looked monstrous and aggressive.

"Well, Fawcett," the Rector said, "I should have known you anywhere. Even with that beard. Would you have known *me?*"

Mr. Fawcett hesitated and recovered. "Yes— I should have known you. You are not—much —changed. Filled out a little, perhaps."

But you could see he didn't mean it. He wouldn't have known Clement Chamberlain through the flesh that had transformed him. The young Clement Chamberlain had been handsome and slender. The Rector of Queningford was still handsome in the style of an epicure of the Roman Empire, but slender he was not.

He looked at his old friend and thought. "Just the same. Amiability itself. I can do what I like with him." He had always done what he liked with Wildon Fawcett.

And young Cartwright looked at Wildon Fawcett and thought:

"Feebleness itself. He'll never stand up to him."

The Rector was trying to bridge over this moment of mutual inspection when Gladys announced suddenly,

"Miss Hilda Wrinch."

Miss Hilda Wrinch strode into the room with her air of impetuous purpose. She was not to be diverted by the presentation of Mr. Wildon Fawcett. In the act of grasping his hand she addressed herself sideways to the Rector.

"They want you," she said, "to come and look at the decorations."

"Presently, my dear Miss Wrinch, presently."

"Presently'll be too late. There won't be any light to see them by."

"But I'm engaged for the moment with Mr. Fawcett."

"Has he—has he got to catch a train or anything?"

"No. He's only just come."

"If he's only just come you must have got hours, and it won't take you five minutes. You might bring Mr. Fawcett along, too."

"You're a very persistent young lady."

"I should think I *was* persistent. It takes persistence to decorate a church that's miles too big for any decorations. You asked us to do it and the very least you can do is to come and look

at them. Don't you think so, Mr. Cart-
right?"

"I'm not taking any sides. But I'll come if
you ask me."

"I do ask you. Now you're *all* coming. You
needn't look at me like that, Canon Chamberlain.
Miss Lambert's made a masterpiece of the altar
rails and pulpit, and you've got to come and say
how wonderful it is. She won't like it if you
don't."

And they went. After all, the Rector, once
fairly aroused from his arm-chair, was not sorry
to show off the beautiful church to his old friend,
not sorry to show off his devoted band of work-
ers. Even Miss Wrinch was devoted. How
that girl worked. Miles and miles of visiting
she had saved him.

A track in the shrubbery beside the house led
to a wicket gate that opened on the graveyard.
They went up a flagged path between the tombstones, seventeenth century tombstones, shaped
like tea caddies, with heavy carved festoons, long
tombstones with fluted cylindrical tops, upright
tombstones, showing the death's head and cross-
bones, showing the cherub's head and trumpet.
Standard roses, still sparsely blooming, bordered
the walks.

They saw the church, the great grey nave anchored out among the tombstones, with its upper deck of clerestory, its tall, wide windows, its row of gargoyles, grey, sinuous animal forms squatting head downwards under the long roof, the square, decorated lantern tower, perfect as on the day when the builder carved the last curling leaf on the last pinnacle.

They entered through the south door.

Hilda was right. The church was too big for the decorations; too perfect. At first they were aware of nothing but the great windows. The solid walls had become a delicate grey framework for the windows; they showed insubstantial in the rich, stained light, holding up sheet after sheet of coloured and translucent flame. Figures of saints in robes of blue and green, crimson and petunia, standing under pale gold canopies. Panes that might have been sliced from blocks of sapphire and emerald, ruby, amethyst and topaz, patch-worked by the thick black veining of the lead. The low September sunshine lit up the immense west window of the Last Judgment, where St. Michael and the resurrection divided the thin gold and white of the blessed spirits from the savage blood-red fires of hell.

Mr. Fawcett stood with his mouth open, trying to disentangle angels from devils and damned souls from the souls of the blessed. The Rector observed with satisfaction his attitude of awe. A personal satisfaction. He could still see the beauty of his church, and was proud of it, though he could no longer feel it. He was like a husband who has no more passion for his wife yet finds pleasure in watching her effect on other men.

They turned and discovered behind the carved oak screen, in the dim light of the chancel, the softly moving figures of the devotees, Miss Lambert and Miss Minchin and the two Ballinger girls from the King's Head. They then saw that the pulpit was wearing crimson streamers on an under dress of misty white, Virginia creeper and old man's beard, and that an enormous pumpkin had come to rest at its base in a bed of barley ears, red apples and brown pears.

But not yet did the Rector turn his attention to the decorations. Pride, pride in his church, in the beautiful thing of which he had lordship and possession, pride filled him. Here was he, Rector of St. Mary's the Virgin, Queningford, perhaps the most perfect specimen of pure Fifteenth Century architecture in England, and here was Fawcett, his friend, who had only in twenty

years succeeded in being curate of St. Simon
and St. Jude's, a sooty modern Gothic horror in
the slums of Bristol. And this pride as it swelled
up in him reminded him of his War Memorial
(he now definitely thought of it as his). He
must tell Fawcett about the War Memorial.

He drew him aside and showed him the site
he had fixed for it, that bit of bare wall beside
the south door. Tablet under a canopy—The
men's names—His thought—Consecration—The
Church the proper guardian of their memories—
Decorated Gothic of the Fifteenth Century—All
in perfect keeping.

And Mr. Fawcett sighed a thick sigh and
murmured: "Wonderful thought, Chamberlain.
Beautiful thought." In fact he behaved so like
Miss Lambert that the Rector was more than
ever assured; a male Miss Lambert was exactly
what he wanted.

But Miss Wrinch was at his side. She whispered sharply: "Praise the pulpit." She put her
large, forcible hand on his arm and led him away
from the spot destined for the War Memorial.

Miss Lambert stood by her masterpiece, the
pulpit. Her head was a little on one side, she
was contemplating her final touch, a bunch of
black-purple grapes that, slung from the candle-

sticks, lay on the breast of the pulpit like a huge
pendant.

The Rector smiled. For one moment he had
a vision of himself rising up out of the Virginia
creeper and old man's beard as out of an enormous crinoline. Instantly he dragged back his
flippant fancy. The smile became a smile of
grave, of almost tender benevolence; Miss Lambert's reward.

"This is *your* work?" The stress implied
that it could have been nobody else's.

"Mine. *And* the altar rails."

"It is very beautiful. You must indeed have
worked hard!"

She smiled the smile of an ecstatic.

"Do you approve of the bunch of grapes? It
was an after thought."

"It is absolutely right. Ab-so-lutely."

"I thought," she said, "that the symbolism
would be clear. You see that the bunch is shaped
like a heart. Our Lord's heart. His blood and
the vine."

"I see. I see. Very beautiful. *Very* beautiful."

"I've carried out the same idea for the altar
rail. If you have time to look at it."

"All the time in the world."

He followed her down the chancel. Miss Lambert, in passing, waved her hand towards the choir stalls.

"Dear Hilda's work," she said.

Miss Wrinch had festooned the choir stalls with rich, thick ropes of flowers, fruit and leaves, a della Robbia effect. The Rector made no comment, and as if his silence had gratified her, by the time they came to the altar rail Miss Lambert's smile was more ecstatic than ever, and before she spoke again she made a little purring noise in her throat, a happy murmur.

The altar rail was finished off with a border of vine leaves and bunches of little grapes, green and purple. A row of little wheatsheaves stood up under them.

"Suitable," she said, "to the Sacrament. Corn and vine. Bread and wine."

For a moment she stood before her work, entranced, not with the joy of the artist, but with the rapture of the saint; the mystic thrilled by the symbol, her soul yearning, reaching out from the symbol to the divine reality behind it. To-morrow, in the freshness of the morning, fasting, she would kneel before that altar rail, before her vine leaves and her grapes, she would drink the blood of the vine and eat the bread of the wheat, she would drink Christ's blood and eat his body. Canon Chamberlain would give them to her; he would stand behind the altar rail wearing his best stole, the white and gold one, he would stoop down to her and give her the cup and the bread, and the words that he spoke then he would speak to her only. And because of her vine-leaves and her grapes she would feel that she was a sort of priestess, helping him to administer the Sacrament.

And while Miss Lambert stood before the altar rail and dreamed, Miss Wrinch, wandering into the chancel with young Cartwright, came upon a long ribbon of Virginia creeper lying on the floor.

"What's that for?" he said.

"To go along the top of Miss Lambert's pulpit. I wish," she said viciously, "it was holly leaves, to prick him."

"You mustn't," he said. He was loyal.

"I must or I shall burst. First it's the War Memorial, and now it's you. Everybody wants you to stay and nobody wants that Fawcett man. But he wants you to go, and you're going. Just because you tried to wake him up."

"No. No. He wants me to go because it'll be better for me, better for the work. After all,

I'm young and strong. I've no business to be holding on to a cushy job. It's like the war, you know."

"All the same, that isn't what he's thinking of. You know it isn't."

Young Cartwright set his face hard.

"He's my chief," he said, "till I've left him. If only I could believe that the other beggar would do my job all right. But, between ourselves, he looks a regular slacker. I expect I shall find St. Simon and St. Jude's in no end of a mess."

"You'll like that. You like cleaning up messes."

"Well, it does seem to be my job," he said and paused. "Look here, if you can get those boys to stick to it at Kempston, I wish you would."

"I'll try. What's more I won't leave *him* alone. I'll think of things for him to do, and come round and worry him till he does them. I'll find all the nastiest things in the parish, the things he hates most—like going to see people with sore throats—and make him do them. He thinks he'll have an easier time when you're gone; but he won't; he'll have a devil of a time."

"Don't, Hilda. He'll hear you."

"I don't care if he does. But he won't. He can't hear anybody but Miss Lambert."

He hadn't heard her, but Miss Minchin, spreading vegetable marrows round the reading-desk, had heard and wondered, and Mr. Fawcett, creeping round to look at the della Robbia choirstalls, had heard. And from that moment he conceived a feeling for Miss Wrinch which would have been dislike if the lovable little man could have disliked anybody.

Presently Canon Chamberlain and young Cartwright and Mr. Fawcett gathered together and went out.

And Miss Lambert, a little depressed after her ecstasy, was left with Hilda and Miss Minchin.

"Hilda dear," she said, "would you mind telling dear Miss Minchin to be careful how she places those vegetable marrows. I'm afraid they'll trip the Rector up."

"Serve him jolly well right, too, for firing Cartwright out."

"Oh, Hilda—He has his reasons."

"Rotten bad ones."

"My dear—we're in the church. . . . If he catches his cassock in the carrots. . . . I shall have to speak to her myself." She hesitated.

"Why don't you?"

"Because I don't want her to think me disagreeable."

"You don't mind her thinking me disagreeable."

"She wouldn't."

"What you really mean is, you don't want her to think you're cocky because your pulpit knocks spots out of her reading desk."

And that was what Miss Lambert had meant. The Rector had praised her pulpit and her altar rails and he had said nothing at all to poor Miss Minchin. In her hour of triumph she didn't want to seem over-exalted and to criticize Miss Minchin. All the same, if the Rector tripped over the vegetable marrow, or if he caught his cassock in the carrots that supported the turnips, and the turnips and the vegetable marrow were to start rolling down the centre aisle——

She spoke to Miss Minchin who replied acidly that the vegetable marrow and the carrots would do very well where they were, and that the Rector wasn't fool enough (as if Miss Lambert had said he was!) to catch his foot in anything, and that Miss Lambert had better finish her pulpit before the light went.

And Miss Lambert, feeling very sorry for

A CURE OF SOULS

Miss Minchin, and saying to herself that jealousy was the hardest thing she had to contend with in this parish, finished her pulpit.

CHAPTER XI

IT was mid-October. The curates had gone.
And all over the Rectory and in the mind of
the Rector there was stillness and the peace of
God. No fear that Cartwright would come
thundering into the study in his big boots and
sling a plan at him, and rouse him up out of his
blessed state. No fear that he would come in
and find Jackman huddled in an arm-chair and
writhing with the torture of his soul. Nothing
more than an occasional visit from Wildon Fawcett, dropping in to lunch or tea, and enjoying
both like a healthy Christian, with a proper appreciation of the gifts of the good kind God; so
different from Cartwright's bumptious indiffer-
ence and Jackman's sick austerity.

They talked; they talked about things that interested Canon Chamberlain; about French politics; about the possibility or impossibility of
making Germany pay; about the probable action
of America, the prospects of a General election,
the latest utterance of the Dean of St. Paul's,

and the deplorable influence of the Nonconformists in Queningford. Only on the subject of Nonconformists did Mr. Fawcett show signs of uncharitable feeling. Then his mild face hardened and a sudden inimical light darted from his milk-blue eyes. They talked about a Nonconformist as if it were some abominably illbehaved animal that had got into the room. "Queningford," Canon Chamberlain said, "stinks with dissent." And Mr. Fawcett turned down the corners of his mouth as if he were well aware of it.

"The trouble is," said Canon Chamberlain, "that I have to order my bacon from the Stores. Withers keeps better bacon than Parker, but of course one can't deal with him."

"Of course not," said Mr. Fawcett and remembered that the only grocer in Kempston was a Baptist. "Not if you can go elsewhere."

He agreed with everything Canon Chamberlain said. He thought him, and showed that he thought him, the wisest and the best of men. No fear of Mr. Fawcett starting an idea of his own or suggesting that the Canon should entertain any idea that was not his own. You couldn't conceive Mr. Fawcett getting up a fife and drum band. Why, he hadn't even approached the sub-

A CURE OF SOULS

ject of the evening classes; and the Rector hoped
that, if only you could keep him in his state of
innocence, he never would.

Sometimes he brought his wife, a little dry
woman, prematurely grey, who agreed with
everything Mr. Fawcett said, which was the
same thing as agreeing with Canon Chamberlain.
She praised Fuller's matchless cooking.

"So different from what we have to put up
with at Kempston. My husband *does* appreciate good things." And sometimes she would
beg for the recipe of an unusual dish, thinking
that they would have it the day the Rector came
to luncheon with them at Kempston, if he ever
did. (He went once, but never again. Never in
his life had he eaten anything so horrible as the
Fawcetts' luncheon. He couldn't have believed
that such things could be. It made him feel ill
only to think of it. No wonder that Fawcett and
his wife were hardly ever well.)

But though hardly ever well, they did their
parish visiting so thoroughly that it wasn't necessary for him to take Kempston on his rounds,
except when he wanted to call on Mrs. Hancock. And as Miss Wrinch on her motor bike
accounted for the outlying districts, and Miss
Lambert, in her devotion, called on every poor

person in Queningford once a fortnight, it was no longer necessary for him to go from house to house there. Nay more, he had no need of a second curate to do it for him. Miss Lambert could take over the parish work of any curate. She had fulfilled her promise to relieve him of the greater burden. And when he thought of that fragile lady, tramping from door to door, and sitting in shut rooms that smelt of labourers' clothes and unwashed skin, performing all those duties which he shrank from most, he reassured himself with the thought that Southwark must have been much worse. The fact that Miss Lambert had been paid for Southwark didn't enter into his calculations any more than it entered into hers. When he felt disinclined to take two Services on a Sunday he sent for Mr. Markham of Moulton who had no living and took pupils. And so, having saved his senior curate's salary, he engaged a butler who would valet him and a first-rate gardener who would look after the vegetables and fruit. He would improve his hot-houses and grow better grapes.

And his mornings moved on again, calm and unhurrying, to lunch time; calm and unhurrying, his afternoons moved on to tea-time and to dinner. He read his *Morning Post,* his *Specta-*

tor, his *Nineteenth Century,* his *Punch* and his *Church Times,* he read the books that came down in the box from Mudie's, novel after novel, and *Memoirs* and *Reminiscences* (he liked them mildly scandalous); he lunched and he dined at the Manor; he drove himself about in his governess cart from one rich, comfortable house to another; he went to tea with Mrs. Hancock. He gave little luncheons and dinners and tea parties in return, sorting his guests with wisdom and care, never mixing the social shades wrong, so that nothing in the least unpleasant ever happened.

And he made a point of asking Miss Lambert to stay for tea every Friday when she came to give what she called an account of her stewardship. He had reason to believe that this weekly communion stimulated zeal. And there was something very soothing in Miss Lambert's gentle ardour after the devastating explosions of Cartwright and Jackman.

No. He didn't know what he would do without Miss Lambert and her devotion, or even without Miss Wrinch. To be sure, the younger lady had a way of sending him off on wild goose chases to the farthest limits of the parish, to see sick people who when he got there turned out not to have been sick at all. But he put this down to her youth and inexperience, and took care to verify the facts before he allowed himself to be drawn another time.

November came. Two weeks ago the Rector's calendar had shown him that Charlotte and Daphne were due to visit him in mid-October. He wrote, asking them for the first week in November. Thus, out of all time to be, he had saved two weeks of blessed life.

But at the end of the first week in November they came. They were to stay a fortnight. A fortnight was the extreme limit of his endurance.

All his life he had turned his great natural resources, imagination, ingenuity, and a thorough knowledge of human behaviour, to the protection of his peace; and hitherto he had contrived to save it from any grave disturbance. He had now to arrange matters so that Charlotte and Daphne wouldn't care to stay longer than a fortnight, if as long. The time and the weather were propitious, November setting in rainy and cold and grey. He had already reckoned on the absence of the Philpots and one or two other county families, and the cessation of social activity in Queningford. But absence was not enough. He must gather together such presences as would prove deterrent. He owed hospitality to Miss Lambert, Miss Minchin, old Mrs. Filkins, the Fawcetts and several other profoundly uninteresting people. He had told Charlotte that Queningford was the dullest place on earth; he would prove it to her by asking them to meet her. Thus he would kill three birds with one stone; he would pay off his social debts; he would have Charlotte's and Daphne's help in entertaining his difficult guests; and he would have destroyed in Charlotte and in Daphne all desire to visit Queningford again. Not that he worked deliberately with this intent; his mind moved by instinct rather than by calculation, and it was after his arrangements had been made that he reflected, not without satisfaction, that such would be their probable result.

The motor car from the King's Head brought Charlotte and Daphne from the station in time for lunch. The Rector came out into his porch to meet them. He gave his hand to Charlotte, who sat heavily, and heaved her up out of the car. Daphne jumped out in the lightness and slenderness of her youth. He saw a delicious round chin resting on a fur collar, a smiling geranium mouth, a soft little Roman nose, cheeks

only less vivid than the mouth, soft and young,
brown eyes that twinkled at him under her dark
felt hat. Daphne was charming.

She cried out in her high girl's voice, "Hello,
Uncle Clement!" and gave him geraniums to
kiss.

If only Daphne could have come without her
mother. And yet, what should he have done
with her? The two could at least talk to each
other. Charlotte Roper was forty-five and stout;
she had the Chamberlain face, the long Chamberlain cheeks, the long, low Roman nose, the
wide Chamberlain mouth, sinuous, sensuous,
cynical. This face was coloured a uniform apple
brown and had little eyes like lizards darting and
turning all the time.

"Is that your car?" she said.

"No. No. I have to hire."

Charlotte looked disappointed; and Daphne,
as if she found her mother's eagerness disgust-
ing, tried to cover it up.

"I say, what a jolly house you've got."

"I'm glad you like it," he said with his half-
ironic politeness, and led the way to that drawing-room whose perfection would intimate to
Charlotte and Daphne that he had no need of
woman's beautifying and refining hand.

"Topping room," was Daphne's simple comment.

Charlotte lowered herself into the most comfortable chair, which happened to be *his* chair. He could see the little lizard eyes running about, darting into corners, seizing on details, envious, appraising. She had nothing like this in her flat in West Kensington. Really, in the division of the furniture, their mother might have left *some* of the best pieces to her. Clement knew what he was about when he gave a home to their mother and her furniture in Gloucester. It paid to be always on the spot. He must have ear-marked the best things and told her what he would like to have. And of course he had them. Clement had always had everything he wanted. If their mother hadn't spoiled him he wouldn't be the mass of selfishness he was now.

"You certainly do know how to make yourself comfortable," she said.

"Why shouldn't he?" said Daphne.

"I never said he shouldn't."

"No, but you looked it," said the truthful girl.

"To be comfortable yourself is the way to make other people comfortable," said Clement.

"I see," said Charlotte, "that's why you do it."

"It's certainly one reason why I do it."

"Anyhow, you've bagged the easiest chair in the room, mother."

"Quite right, Charlotte. And that isn't the way to talk to your mother, Daphne."

"Oh, mother's used to my ragging, aren't you, Mum?"

"Politeness would surprise me more, if that's what you mean."

They would go on like that, answering each other back with their silly chaff, for hours on end. He knew them. He couldn't think of anything more tiresome.

"I'm perfectly polite to Uncle Clement," said Daphne, keeping it up. "Aren't I?"

"Perfectly. You might remember that your mother is my sister."

"Oh, but I want her to feel at home."

"I think," the Rector said, "we might have lunch."

"That's a good idea," said Daphne.

How good it was she realised when lunch was served. The Rector, half amused, watched the young animal as she bit with strong white teeth into the jam puffs and cheese biscuits. Her cheeks glowed with pleasure. He liked Daphne.

Charlotte, too, was not indifferent. He respected Charlotte.

When lunch was over he showed them his house, a long, rambling expedition. Charlotte insisted that all closed doors should be opened to her; he opened them, shrugging his shoulders in mild wonder at her curiosity, letting it have its way. She even burst into the kitchen and compelled him to introduce her to Fuller. Charlotte made a point of being friendly with the servants in the houses where she stayed, whereby her comfort was considerably increased. So now she complimented Fuller on the excellence of her jam puffs and the beauty of her shining pans. Charlote's nose, as Fuller said afterwards, was everywhere. "She'd 'a bin through the scullery door like lightning if I 'adn't stood with my back to it o' purpose. Spying, I call it."

"She'll not stay more than her fortnight," Gladys said.

"Nor be arst again in no 'urry, she won't."

When Charlotte had seen all there was to be seen they settled down in the study. Daphne examined the bookcases while the Rector and his sister talked. Charlotte wanted to know how many servants it took to run the place. He enumerated: butler, cook-housekeeper, parlourmaid and housemaid. A stableman outside and a gardener. Six.

"I could do it with one house-parlourmaid and one man," said Charlotte.

"So could I. But I shouldn't like it. No more would you."

"Oh *me*. I'm quite content with my little flat. It only takes one maid, and a charwoman once a week. I know where I am."

"And I," said the Rector, "know where I am not." He could see what Charlotte was driving at, trying to make him feel uncomfortable by contrasting his way of living with her own. And she was quite well off, too.

"It's all right," said she, "as long as you can afford it."

"My dear Charlotte, have you ever known me do anything I couldn't afford?"

"No. I must say I haven't. What are you doing there, Daphne?"

"Exploring," Daphne said.

He looked round uneasily. He remembered Flaubert and Maupassant. But Daphne was at the upper shelves.

"Running amuck among my Christian Fathers, are you?"

Daphne giggled.

"And *now*," said Charlotte, with an air of really beginning, "tell me all about your work."

"I won't. You know parish work doesn't interest you."

"No. But it interests me to think of you doing it."

"Why not me?"

"Because, of all the jobs that you detest most —visiting poor people, especially when they've got things the matter with them—what can you do for them?"

"That reminds me." He rang the bell.

Pridget appeared.

"Oh, Pridget, you might tell Fuller to make some soup for Mrs. Mabbit. Good strong soup. They'll send for it tomorrow morning."

"Very good, sir. Good strong soup."

"That's one thing at least," he said, "that I can do for them."

"For their bodies. But how do you manage about their souls? I always *have* wondered, Clement, how you manage about their souls."

"Mercifully," said Clement, "it is not left to me."

"You mean you've got curates."

"No. No." He was abstracted. He could hear Daphne fumbling softly behind his chair.

"I mean that there are the Church Services and the Church Sacraments."

"I see, you just let them loose among them."

"You know, Charlotte, that I do not mean that."

He would have liked to say something about God's grace being sufficient for them, only somehow you couldn't talk about God's grace to Charlotte.

A squeal of joy from Daphne cut Charlotte short.

"Oh—oh—oh—Uncle Clement! Naughty!"

She rose from behind his chair holding up a book: *Madame Bovary*.

There was a moment of discomfort. He recovered.

"You don't mean to say you've read it?"

"No. But I'm going to. I've heard of it."

"My dear child. I really think you'd better not."

"Why not? If it's fit reading for a clergyman of the Church of England, it's fit reading for me."

"What does your mother say?"

"Mother jolly well knows it's no good her saying anything."

"Is that true, Charlotte?"

"Daphne knows that if I don't say anything

it's because I trust her. You needn't worry, Clement. She'll throw it away if it's nasty."

"Flaubert's all right," said Daphne. "It's Maupassant——"

Over the back of the chair, where Charlotte couldn't see him, he made a desperate signal to Daphne to spare him and respect the secret of the green curtain.

"Maupassant? You haven't got Maupassant there?" cried Charlotte.

Daphne whispered, "All right, old thing, I won't give you away. . . . I *haven't* read Maupassant, mother."

She curled up on the floor with *Madame Bovary* and Charlotte returned to the parish as if there had been no interruption.

"How many curates does it take to run it?"

"I *had* two."

"Unmarried?"

"Unmarried."

"Young?"

"Young."

"What's become of them?"

"Oh, they've gone."

"Why on earth did you let them go? They might have amused Daphne."

"*What's* that about me and curates, mother?"

"Cartwright might have amused Daphne, but I'm not so sure about Jackman. He was a solemn chap."

"Well, you can't run a parish like this without curates."

"I can run it with one."

"Oh, you've got *one,* then."

"Yes, but he's forty-five and married. *He* wouldn't amuse Daphne. I told you it was a dull place."

"Oh, well, we knew that. It was *you* we came to see, Clement."

"Thank you. It's very good of you, Charlotte. I wish I could do more for you now you're here."

Charlotte meditated.

"Why didn't you stick to Gloucester?"

"Too many clergymen about."

"As if you weren't one yourself."

"That's why. I don't care to be surrounded with caricatures of myself."

"Anything else?"

"No house. No garden."

"It's a good living, this?"

"Fair."

But how fair it was he did not say. He knew Charlotte was trying to get out of him the precise amount of his income. He hated people who tried to get things out of him.

Then Charlotte said a dreadful thing.

"Daphne, if you've found a book, dear, you might run away and read it in the drawing-room. I want to *talk* to your Uncle."

That meant that everything up to now had been only the preliminary skirmish preparatory to the great attack.

"Why banish her? She's not doing any harm."

"Do as I tell you, dear." And Daphne did as she was told.

Then Charlotte settled down to it.

"Clement," she said, "I can't think how you can bear to live all by yourself in this great barrack of a place."

"It isn't a great barrack. It's rather beautifully proportioned."

She went on, ignoring the contradiction. "Without a chick or a child."

"I don't *want* a child. And what on earth should I do with a chick?"

"Not even a cat or a dog."

"I don't like dogs, and I abominate cats."

Pause. Charlotte's pauses terrified him. He could tell by the indrawn, brooding look of her eyes that her mind, instead of exploring the present and the future, was raking in the past. He wondered what it would bring up. Something disagreeable, you might be sure.

"Did you know that Alice Vachell's married?"

He winced visibly. If there was one name that he was afraid of hearing, one subject that he wished to be buried for all eternity, it was Alice Vachell. Charlotte, with her abominable instinct, had hit on the one supremely disagreeable thing. He knew that she was looking at him sharply, furtively, to see how he took it.

He tried to take it casually, as a thing of no special interest.

"Is that so?" he said.

"Yes. And very happily married, too. She's Mrs. Cecil Thompson and she's got two thumping fat babies, I hear."

His mind went back and back, ten years back to the time of his last curacy. He saw Alice Vachell in her white, thin beauty, growing whiter and thinner as the months went on and nothing was said, though everything was understood. Yes. He supposed there had been something like an understanding. He had been in love with Alice Vachell. He supposed it was love, that feeling which made him want to be always with her. And he had been just on the edge of it, he remembered; the day that Alice had come in after one of their long walks and he had seen her white face suddenly turn whiter, a sick, terrifying whiteness; he had seen her pale mouth, half-open, panting; and oh, how slowly and feebly she had dragged herself upstairs. After that there had been no more long walks and Alice lay about on sofas, looking awful; and the doctor came. And he had been frightened. He couldn't take the risk of having an invalid wife on his hands all his life. He hated illness, and it wasn't as if he was a rich man. So he gave up his curacy and went away, flying, as he put it, from temptation. Then had come Gloucester; then Queningford, and he was almost a rich man. But he had not seen nor heard of Alice Vachell till today. He had tried not to think of her.

It was so like Charlotte to bring it all up again when it had been forgotten.

"Is she stronger than she used to be?" he asked.

His mind clung desperately to his old belief in Alice Vachell's illness. It had been his excuse for leaving her.

"She was never anything but strong when *I* knew her."

"I thought she was supposed to have something mysterious the matter with her. Heart or something."

"I always wondered why you didn't marry her. I suppose that was why."

"There were a great many reasons why."

"Well, if you wanted to marry her, my dear, you were very nicely sold. She had nothing the matter with her. Nothing mysterious. Any fool could have seen what it was."

"What was it?"

"The poor girl was in love with you, that was all."

"I didn't know it."

"Then you were a bigger fool than I took you for. Everybody else knew it. And say what you like you were in love yourself."

Was he? Was he?

"I don't *know*," he said, "that I was."

"I knew. And *she* knew. You ought to have married her, Clement. It would have been the best day's work you ever did."

"It would have been a tremendous risk."

"Oh, well, if you won't ever take a sporting chance."

"Pretty poor sport. It would have been risking her happiness as well as mine."

"I suppose it would, since you were such a coward. Anyhow, she's happy now."

"I'm very glad to hear it."

But he was not glad to hear it. He had not thought about Alice Vachell for years; but in the days when he did still think about her he had thought of her as unmarried. She was kept virgin for his thoughts by her mysterious malady. And the idea of a married Alice, a robust Alice, Alice a Mrs. Cecil Thompson with two thumping fat babies, was not agreeable to him. And there was an element of irony in it. He had been, as Charlotte put it in her gross way, nicely sold. Alice should have remained forever white and thin, justifying him.

"You ought to get married yourself, Clement."

Now it was not to Charlotte's interest that he should marry, since he had money and furniture to leave. Therefore Charlotte was simply pursuing an unpleasant theme for sheer love of unpleasantness.

"I believe in a celibate clergy," he said. "I agree with St. Paul that marriage is good, but celibacy is better."

"Marriage would be the best thing for *you*. Stir you up. You don't take enough exercise, my dear, and I'm sure you eat and drink a great deal more than's good for you. You're getting fat."

He got up. Charlotte had gone too far. She had provoked him beyond endurance. But he was not going to gratify her by showing that he was provoked.

"Supposing," he said sweetly, "we go and see what Daphne's doing."

CHAPTER XII

WHEN he opened the study door, he knew. Daphne had discovered the piano. She was playing a gay dance tune that went

> Di-dump, di-dumpetty,
> Dumpetty, dumpetty,
> Dumpty, dumpty-day.

One of those tunes that you can never get away from, that lodge in the memory and torment it to the end of time. He would hear Daphne's tune when he lay in bed at night and when he woke in the morning; he would hear it in his bath; it would come between him and his prayers: he would hear it when he was writing his sermon and when he was administering the Sacrament and visiting the dying. Di-dump, di-dumpetty. In all the unspeakably solemn moments of his existence it would be with him. Dumpty, dumpty-day. It was the kind of tune he would never have allowed in the house if he could have helped it.

But when he saw Daphne playing it, her body

bowing gracefully to the rhythm and her little hands leaping and pouncing on the keyboard, he hadn't the heart to tell her for goodness' sake to stop that awful row. He could do nothing but think what an infernal nuisance she was. Only when Charlotte, with her skirts turned up above her knees, had established herself before the fire and was knitting, under the cover of the tune he invited Daphne to come with him and see the church. She rose eagerly, rejoiced to hear that there was anything to see; and they went out together. He hoped that Charlotte, as the warmth penetrated her legs, would be too comfortable to get up and follow them.

Daphne greeted the old tomb-stones with little cries of joy. ("Oh, Uncle Clement, wouldn't you *love* to be buried under that tea-caddy one?") But before the beauty of the windows she was silent and grave. She slipped her hand under his arm and gave it a gentle squeeze that showed her pleasure. He looked at her serious, transfigured face and wondered how this could possibly be Daphne, Charlotte's daughter. And the beauty of his church was alive to him again, he felt again the forgotten thrill of his old joy in beauty, started by the little excited hand on his arm.

At last he spoke.

"Uncle Clement, you *do* love it?"

"Yes, Daphne; I love it."

"I love you for loving it."

They stood a moment side by side in their communion, and then moved on quietly. When they had seen all the windows, west and east, north aisle and south aisle and clerestory, she drew him to the organ in the chancel.

"Can you play on it?" she said.

"A little, not very well."

"Play to me."

They went back to the Rectory and found Scarrott, the stableman, and made him come and blow.

And Clement Chamberlain played to her; he played slow, solemn marches, tranquil sentimental voluntaries: he played such music as dies along the aisles and under the high chancel roof to the sound of feet going out of church.

He stopped.

She said, "Go on; oh, *do* go on. It's heaven."

He looked at her. Daphne's soul dreamed in her enchanted eyes. Surely he couldn't have been playing so badly? He started a Bach fugue, gave it up, sighed, and said he was no good. He might have been, only he never practised; he was much too lazy; that was the truth, Daphne.

He struck a loose chord or two. The sounds died away and he heard over his shoulder the voice of Charlotte.

"So *this* is where you're hiding, you two."

She had come to see the church windows.

And they went round again and looked at the windows. But this time it was different. Daphne was different. She laughed at the damned souls and at the little devils of the Last Judgment, and at the sad mutilation of Eve, and the expression on the face of the Queen of Sheba. Her mother's presence had a bad effect on Daphne. It brought out everything that was flippant and vulgar and impudent in her. And she had been adorable when they were alone together. He could see her standing beside him with her face grave and silent before the beauty of the windows; he could hear her asking him if he loved it, and telling him it was heaven when he played. Daphne had a soul, a soul that as long as she lived with Charlotte would never have a chance.

He ought to get her away from her mother for a while, to ask her to stay by herself for a long while; to make her read good books and play good music. He ought to be the noble, refining influence in her life, to encourage her little soul to come out and show itself and grow. He might even take her abroad with him on his next holiday, take her to Florence and Rome and let her see the great buildings, the great statues, the great pictures; satisfy her passion for beauty. And in return Daphne would love him.

But he knew that he would do none of these things.

Next afternoon was the afternoon of the tea-party. It began early. By four o'clock old Mrs. Filkins, the Fawcetts, Miss Minchin and Miss Lambert had arrived. They sat round the golden brown Chippendale table in stiff attitudes, looking queer and out of keeping with the Rector's perfect furniture.

Half-way through the meal, Miss Lambert's face reminding him of the parish, he thought of Mrs. Mabbitt. He rang the bell and the order went forth a second time.

"Pridget, while I remember, you might tell Fuller to make some more soup for Mrs. Mabbitt. Strong and good."

"Uncle Clement'll swim to heaven on seas of soup," Daphne said. "He does let his little light shine before men, doesn't he?"

Miss Lambert looked as if she thought it was on the wings of an angel that he would go. She was sitting next to Charlotte and it was to Charlotte that she poured out his praise. Her voice was so low that he couldn't hear it where he sat apart.

"The light he lets shine is nothing to the light he hides. Nobody who doesn't go among the poor here has any idea of his kindness, his thought. I assure you there's not one poor person in this parish, Mrs. Roper, who's allowed to go hungry."

Charlotte's mouth twitched, folding and unfolding like the mouth of a tortoise. Her little eyes twinkled cruelly. She knew what was the matter with Miss Lambert, what the queer throbbing of her voice meant and the tender yearning in her eyes. The little wavering smile of meekness and of holiness meant the same thing. There was nothing secret in Miss Lambert that Charlotte did not know. She wondered what on earth she should say to the absurd woman.

"Hunger," she said, *"would* appeal to him." She said it for Clement's understanding and her own amusement. She knew she was safe. Miss Lambert, carried away in her ecstacy, would never see the sharp point of it.

"If you knew, Mrs. Roper, what this parish was like before he came, you'd marvel at the change there is."

"I probably should," said Charlotte, and Miss Lambert's holy voice went on.

"Miss Minchin knows what it was like in the old Rector's time."

She was sorry for Miss Minchin, sitting out in the cold without anything to say. Holiness suggested that it would be kind to draw her into the conversation. But Miss Minchin wasn't to be drawn. Her small, withered little face tightened in an expression of peevish integrity.

"The old Rector was not a wealthy man but he was much loved."

"It isn't wealth, dear Miss Minchin. It's the wonderful personal influence. Our dear late Rector had none."

"Perhaps that's why they loved him," Charlotte said.

"You must *work* for Canon Chamberlain to know what he is," said Miss Lambert.

At that Charlotte's face became so enigmatic that Miss Lambert was disconcerted and turned to Daphne on her other side.

"Have you heard your uncle preach yet, Miss Roper?"

"No. We only came yesterday."

"Well, that's a pleasure in store for you."

"Does it last long?" said Daphne.

"Canon Chamberlain can pack more into ten minutes than most preachers can get into an hour."

Charlotte laughed, "I don't see Clement sitting down to write a sermon that would last an hour. Catch him doing anything so strenuous."

"Don't be frightened, Daphne. It would bore me as much as you," said the Rector, roused from a deplorable conversation with Mrs. Fawcett.

"You don't know," said Miss Lambert to Charlotte, "how strenuous he is."

"My dear Miss Lambert, I've known him longer than you have. I know exactly how strenuous he is."

"You don't know how strenuous *she is*," said the Rector. "You wouldn't believe that she does half my work for me in Queningford."

"I shouldn't be surprised," said Charlotte, "if she did it all."

Miss Lambert's rapturous voice replied, "Oh, but he makes it easy for us.

"How does he make it easy for you?" Charlotte really wondered how. She couldn't imagine Clement making anything easy for anybody but himself. And she took a wicked pleasure in drawing Miss Lambert out.

"By the inspiration that he gives. He strengthens all our hands." It was the Rector's consecrated phrase and she had made it hers.

"He does indeed," said Mr. Fawcett, with mildly eruptive fervour. His attention had completely wandered from old Mrs. Filkins who had been trying for the last five minutes to obtain his sympathy for the neuritis in her left arm.

"Neuritis *or* rheumatism," she went on. "Dr. Lawson won't say which it is. Miss Minchin tells me I should try Curic. But really I don't know whether these patent medicines—Canon Chamberlain, do you know Curic?"

"Curic? Where is it? What is it?"

"A patent medicine. For neuritis and rheumatism."

"Never had either of 'em. *My* patent medicine is fresh fruit every morning before breakfast. Vitamins, you know."

Mrs. Filkins was a little deaf. "Vit—— Spell it, please."

"V-i-t-a-m-i-n-s. Vitamins."

"I can get it at the chemist's I suppose?"

"It's not a medicine. It's—it's *in* the fruit, you know."

But Mrs. Filkins was making a note in her head to order Vitamins at Evans's on her way home.

Daphne, who sat between Miss Lambert and Mrs. Filkins, couldn't bear it any longer. She got up, whispered something to her mother and left the room.

Now as the Rector had the unsociable habit of suppressing all gossip, conversation at the Rectory was sustained with difficulty thus cut off from its natural source. It had turned heavily from Vitamins to the problem, propounded by Miss Lambert, whether parishioners should or should not be dunned for their subscriptions to the Coal and Blanket Club, when Daphne appeared again.

Yes. It *was* Daphne. But she had changed her sober gabardine for a frock of magenta silk with immensely wide skirts, that reached barely below her knees. A long chiffon scarf hung on her arm.

Miss Lambert, Miss Minchin, Mrs. Filkins and the Fawcetts all stared at the young girl at once, with a sort of sacred terror as if they thought that Daphne had gone mad. Miss Lambert whispered to Miss Minchin that Miss Roper was going to recite.

But Daphne was not going to recite. Gladys and Pridget followed her and among them they cleared away rugs, chairs and tables from the middle of the room, leaving a large space of polished floor. Charlotte rose and sat down at the piano. She played, not a dance, not a tune you would have thought anybody could have danced to; yet Daphne danced.

A queer, slow, high stepping dance that followed miraculously all the pauses and hesitations of the tune; her knees raised at right angles to her body, she went round and round the open space; throwing up her scarf in half circles, right and left, and twisting herself sideways, in and out of them, right and left. The music quickened; she threw the scarf now before and behind her, bending forwards and backwards; she trailed it on the floor and played with it, dancing, as a kitten plays with its own tail; she flung it down in a heap and danced up to it and away from it as if it fascinated and frightened her. She danced near and nearer, then stooped suddenly and picked it up and danced away with it, and wound it round her body as she danced; then whirled, unwinding and winding it again. She went faster and faster, spinning on the points of her toes, and the scarf, blown out with

her speed, whirled with her, circling her like a
ring of white cloud.

They looked on, Miss Lambert, Miss Minchin,
Mrs. Filkins and the Fawcetts, with stiff, tightened faces; solemn, disapproving faces, frightened faces, bewildered and offended faces. The
Rector struggled with an epicurean smile and
overcame it.

Then Daphne dropped on her right knee, with
her left leg stretched out before her, the toe
pointing to the floor, and the dance was done.

Nobody said anything, and Daphne began another dance. She took a chrysanthemum from a
vase and played with it, tossing it in the air and
catching it, throwing it on the floor and picking
it up again, swaying with it as if she were the
stalk it grew on. She lifted her white arms in
an arch above her head, the chrysanthemum held
up in her clasped fingers, she raised herself on
the tips of her toes brought close together, and
went on them, backwards and forwards, twinkling and twittering up and down the room. She
stuck the chrysanthemum into her hair and burst
into a savage, high-kicking jig, she shook her
head and shook it, dancing, till the mass of her
dark hair came rolling down; then she bent backwards till it fell sheer from the deep curve of her

body; she span round, faster and faster, and it flew out like an open fan; she bowed forwards till it hung before her face like a veil, and Daphne, curtseying, sank to the floor at her uncle's feet, in the whorl of her bright skirts, wagging her head at him.

"Thank you, Daphne," he said in a queer voice, strained with irony.

Then she sprang up, shook back her hair and laughed out before them all. And one by one they rose and took leave, Miss Lambert, Miss Minchin, Mrs. Filkins and the Fawcetts.

When they were all gone her uncle turned to her. "Daphne," he said, "what on earth did you do it for?"

"Why, to amuse them."

"Nonsense," said her mother, "you did it to amuse yourself."

"Don't look at my motives, look at the result."

"They were not amused," said the Rector. "They were frightened."

"That's all very well. What would *you* have done without me? You hadn't got to talk to them as long as I was dancing and it made them go. They'd be here now if it wasn't for me."

The Rector's stiff mouth relaxed. "I know

why you did it. You were bored. You're a young scamp, Daphne, a wicked young scamp."

Daphne kissed him, and ran away to change her frock. Charlotte closed in on him.

There was no escape.

"Clement," she said, "what have you done to that Lambert woman?"

"Done to her? I've done nothing."

"You must have done something to get her into that state."

"What state?"

"Why, she's in love with you."

"Nonsense. Nothing of the sort."

"My dear, she talks about you as if you were God Almighty. You'd better be careful."

"How?"

"Well, you've got to *show* her."

"Show her?" He was disgusted with Charlotte. She was mistaken if she expected him to rise to her vulgarity. "Show her what?"

"That you aren't taking any."

"Really, Charlotte, you do suggest the most unpleasant things. The poor woman's no more thinking of me than you are yourself."

"Thinking? She's thinking of you from morning till night. She'll go off her head with thinking if you don't take care."

"What am I to do? I must be decent to her. She's the best worker I've got in the parish."

"She wouldn't be if you were a married man, my dear."

"Oh yes, she would."

"She would not. It isn't in human nature. Not in that sort of human nature, any way. You must have made precious poor use of your experience if you think it is. But you don't think it. You're not a fool."

"I may be; but I tell you you're misjudging a perfectly innocent woman. Agnes Lambert is incapable——"

"Don't talk rubbish. Every woman's capable. I never said she wasn't innocent. It isn't a crime to be in love with you. It's *your* innocence I'm not so sure about. I can see you exploiting that poor lady's infatuation for all it's worth. Whipping it up and up; so as to get more and more out of her."

"I assure you she doesn't need whipping up. You don't *know* how that woman can work. If it wasn't for her I should have to keep another curate."

"No wonder you believe in a celibate clergy, Clement."

"You are revoltingly cynical," he said.

"Am I? That's all the thanks I get trying to keep you out of trouble. Well, don't say I didn't warn you."

With that she left him.

She left him profoundly uncomfortable. He told himself he didn't believe a word of it; he knew that Charlotte had been moved as usual by sheer love of unpleasantness for unpleasantness' sake; all the same, her suggestion had made him profoundly uncomfortable.

He began to count the days till Charlotte should be gone. This was Friday. It couldn't happen till next Thursday week. Thirteen more days.

He got through them somehow. In the mornings he was driven into doing parish work to get away from Charlotte. Disagreeable as it was, it was less disagreeable than Charlotte. He secluded himself all Saturday on the ground that he was preparing his sermons. Sunday accounted for itself. He had arranged something, something that would break the strain of Charlotte, for each afternoon of the other days. Monday, it was tea with Mrs. Hancock; Tuesday, tea with Miss Lambert; Wednesday, tea with Miss Minchin before five o'clock service; Thursday, tea with the Fawcetts; Friday was

Miss Lambert's day. Saturday and Sunday were as before; Monday, Mrs. Hancock to tea at the Rectory; Tuesday, tea with Mrs. Filkins (Charlotte and Daphne wouldn't want to come again in a hurry.) On Wednesday he hired the King's Head car and took them to Cirencester. In the evenings he played chess with Charlotte to keep her quiet, while Daphne read or sang or played on the piano.

The last three days he was in an agony lest anything should happen to prevent them going. Charlotte might catch a cold or sprain an ankle. He was very careful to see that she had enough warm things on and that a good fire was kept up in her bedroom, and that she didn't slip getting in and out of the governess cart and car. On Wednesday evening Charlotte terrified him by showing symptoms of a bilious headache, but on Thursday, Providentially, she had recovered.

And they went. He had never liked Charlotte more than in the happy act of her going.

At the last moment it was Daphne who made him uncomfortable. She gave him another sight of her when they stood together in the hall, waiting for Charlotte.

"Uncle Clement, I'm glad we saw those windows by ourselves. It's funny, but it's made me feel as if I knew you better than Mother does."

Did she? Did she know him? Did he not know himself too well who knew that when Daphne was gone it would be years before she came again, and that he would never take her abroad with him and never, never ask her to stay at Queningford by herself? That, in short, he didn't care for her. He cared for nothing in this world but his own peace.

CHAPTER XIII

BUT in going Charlotte had left something of herself behind her. The spirit of Charlotte was in that idea she had put into his head. It was unpleasant; it wouldn't have been Charlotte's idea if it had not been unpleasant; still, he would have dismissed it with contempt, because it was Charlotte's idea, if it had not answered to a vague uneasiness that he had felt lately. He had noticed, he could not help noticing, the increasing exaltation of Miss Lambert's manner. He had put it down to her increasing holiness, but Charlotte had made him see that it was at least open to another interpretation. The poor dear lady *did* treat him rather as if he had been God Almighty. And the last thing he wanted was to be made a God of. He couldn't live up to the part. It exacted too much responsibility, and he hated responsibility. Here again (for not even Charlotte could say that he was fatuous) he had supposed it was his priesthood and not his manhood that she worshipped. But now he couldn't get away from Charlotte's abominable idea.

To be sure its full unpleasantness found no place in his mind; for he couldn't believe, as Charlotte apparently did, that parish work was Miss Lambert's way of making love and that if he didn't take care he would be drawn into marrying her; he didn't believe that marrying had entered into her innocent head any more than it had entered into his. Yet he was afraid, and it would be hard to say what he was afraid of, unless it was of becoming necessary to Miss Lambert, so that he would be the first that she came to in any difficulty or trouble. He knew that women in Miss Lambert's state, if it was her state, were in the habit of inventing difficulties and troubles so as to multiply opportunities for meeting the object of their devotion; and the idea of becoming such an object was very repugnant to him. Suppose Miss Lambert took it into her head to call on him at any hour of the day, how on earth was he to stop it? He might say ten times that he was not at home and the eleventh time she would find him there. What he dreaded more than anything was some scene in which Miss Lambert would show emotion. He couldn't bear people who showed emotion. His great objection to poor Jackman had been that he couldn't control himself.

He ought to take steps to prevent it.

But what steps? What could he do that he had not done? Or what was he doing that he shouldn't do? Well, he was seeing her much too often for one thing. These weekly visits were quite unnecessary. Then he remembered that today was Friday and that Friday was Miss Lambert's day. She would be with him that afternoon, unless he—— Should he send round a note saying that he was engaged? If so, he would have to fix another day, or if he didn't fix it his problem was only put off till next Friday.

Inexorably these Fridays would come round.

No. He must make his stand today. He would see her and give her tea as usual, and he would cut short their communion by pretending that he had to go into Cirencester tomorrow and that consequently he had his sermons to prepare today. After all, his hair did want cutting; he would go into Cirencester tomorrow and have it cut. And before she left he would break it to her that in future he would receive her reports monthly instead of weekly. That, as Charlotte put it, would "show" her.

Easy enough to plan; but horrible to do. The

dear woman was so gentle, so intolerably gentle.
When it came to the awful point, when he
actually said it, said that he thought it was unnecessary to trouble her with these weekly parish reports and that in future he would be content if he were to have them, say, once a month,
he thought for one moment that Miss Lambert
was going to show emotion. Her eyes looked at
him as if he had struck her, wounded, startled
eyes. Then she seemed to gather herself together, determined not to betray herself. And
she answered gently.

She said that she had only thought he wanted
to be kept in touch with the poorer parishioners,
and that to keep him in touch the weekly reports
were necessary. But if he preferred it she would
call monthly.

"Then," he said, "you will have more to tell
me, and your time" (he called it *her* time) "will
not be taken up with unimportant matters. Of
course, if there should be anything urgent you
will let me know."

She promised that if there was anything
urgent she would let him know.

"You can write," he said.

Yes, she could write.

She was holding her mouth tight to keep it

steady, but her eyes quivered. She had a crushed, beaten look, as if he had taken something from her, some joy by which she lived. He was seeing things he never would have seen if it hadn't been for Charlotte. Charlotte had come between them, destroying the simplicity and peace of their relations. He was afraid, terribly afraid that Charlotte, with her instinct for the hidden, had seen something that was there. And he would so much rather not have known that it was there. He felt as if they, he and Charlotte together, had been spying on the poor dear woman. Worse than all, he was afraid that Miss Lambert was going to cry. He didn't know what on earth he should say to her if she cried.

He tried to soften his brutality.

"I'm only thinking what will be best for you," he said. "I want to make your work easier."

But he knew he wasn't making it easier, he was making it heavy, heavier than she could bear.

"Don't think of me," she said. "I only want to make it easier for *you*."

"Easier for both of us, then." He laughed, genially.

And on that she left him, holding out a fragile

hand and withdrawing it suddenly, as if his touch hurt her. He had noticed before that curious gesture.

Yes, there was something.

And now, having once seen it, he could see nothing else. He saw it in her face upturned to him in ecstasy when he gave her the Sacrament, in her eyes fixed on him through the morning and evening Services. It was as if her face was the only face in the church, her eyes the only eyes. He felt them on him all the time. The prayers were his refuge; yet even in the prayers he felt them on him behind the mask of the joined hands. With an extraordinary uneasiness he felt them. He was sensitised, exquisitely, to her presence. It was as if she could get at him by the sheer force of her obsession. He resented this.

His subsequent behaviour was as much an effort to protect himself from Miss Lambert as to protect Miss Lambert from herself. Thus, when he saw her on the other side of the village street, instead of crossing over and engaging her in conversation as he used to do, he would salute her with distant and austere benevolence. November and December passed. He had made no attempt to shorten the term he had set between her visits. Neither had she. She had called once since their last meeting; she had confined herself strictly to the business of the parish, and had left him earlier than the former hour of her departure. He had noticed nothing but an increasing gentleness and holiness of manner. The exaltation and ecstasy had gone. It was as if she herself were marking the distance, setting the tone for all their intercourse; almost as if she had said, "You needn't be afraid. There was nothing in it. If anybody disturbs your peace and comfort it will not be me."

And he was beginning to feel peaceful and comfortable again. Then—it was in January, soon after the New Year—when, coming in after a visit to Mrs. Hancock, he was told that Miss Lambert was waiting for him in the drawing-room. Se had been waiting half an hour.

He went in slowly, reluctantly. He had a terrible premonition of unpleasantness. It wouldn't be an urgent case of sickness in the village. Hitherto, ever since their pact, in cases of urgent sickness Miss Lambert had written. And at the first sight of her he knew that he was in for it. There was going to be emotion, a scene. Miss Lambert's face had changed from its look of inward stillness; it was slightly inflamed, and the skin had a glazed look where tears had left their trail. She had been crying; not only while she waited but before that and many times. Her eyes were hot and brilliant. But she was not crying now. He saw with relief that she was not.

She spoke first; hurriedly, as if she anticipated some word that would be a blow.

"Forgive me for coming. I had to."

"You must forgive *me*," he said. "If I had known you were coming I should not have kept you waiting."

"You said I was to write if there was anything urgent. But—I couldn't write. I had to see you."

"Anything wrong in the parish?"

He knew there wasn't. He was giving himself time, time to adapt himself to this disturbance.

"No. It's nothing in the parish. It's my own trouble. I don't know that I ought to burden you with it, when you have so much to do, so many things to think of——"

He tried to think of the right thing, the inevitable thing, the thing he was expected to say on these occasions. It came glibly to his tongue. He had said it so many times before.

"Surely, surely, that's what I'm here for."

"Yes. If others have their right I think I may have mine. My trouble is more than I can bear any longer by myself. And there is nobody but you, nobody on this earth whom I could tell it to."

"What is this trouble? Let us look at it together. Perhaps it won't seem so very bad."

"I can't think of anything worse. A little while ago, two months ago, I was happy. Happy in my work, happy in myself, more happy than I should have thought it possible to be. I thought this happiness was going to last forever, because I knew the source of it was God."

"Well—if you knew that——"

"Yes, I knew it. I hadn't a doubt."

"And surely," he said, "you don't doubt it now? It isn't doubt?"

"No, I don't doubt it. If I had a shadow of doubt I should understand what has happened to me."

"What—has—happened?"

"It's gone. Gone. All the happiness. All the peace, the wonderful peace. Just as if God had never given it to me. Is it possible that he could take it away after having given it me?"

Oh, he was in for it. Deep, deep in.

"That's not a question you should ask. Try how you can get back to it again."

"But that's the awful thing. I *have* tried and I can't get back. I'm cut off. Cut off from God."

"No soul can be cut off except by its own will."

"Oh, if it was only my own will. How could I possibly will this agony? I can't tell you what that happiness was like. I don't claim to have had *experiences* like the great saints; but I had my certainty. I was conscious, intensely conscious, of the presence of God, I felt him in my prayers, I felt him in the holy Sacrament; I felt that there was nothing between me and God; that I was really and truly one with Him. I was there, resting in a great peace. And I am not there now. I cannot get back."

"You can think of no reason why?"

"I can think of nothing. I never believed more in God, I never loved him more than now that I'm cut off from him."

There was a long, long pause. Again he wondered what he should say to her; his mind went carefully, tentatively, among all its thoughts of God, seeking for the right thought. Surely the right thought was there, somewhere, and he would find it.   He could only think of trivial thoughts, perverse thoughts.   He thought of Miss Lambert's shoes, worn and deformed by her tramping through the parish; he wondered what her age really was and whether it could have anything to do with her present trouble; he remembered odd scraps of medical knowledge that he had picked up here and there; remembered and dismissed them.   He thought of what Charlotte had said of her.   And at that his mind revolted, made a great leap aside, and instantly, miraculously, there flashed on him the thing he wanted.   Something he had read once, before his mind was lazy, in the days when he read so that he might think, instead of reading so that he might not think.

"There was once," he said, "a great thinker, Baruch Spinoza.   He wrote a great book about God.   He said that he who really loves God should not seek that God should love him in return.   Now that is not true.   It is quite right that we should seek that God should love us. But Spinoza's saying is the perversion of a great truth.   And that is that for us the important thing is that we should love God.   And we should not seek to gratify our emotions in our communion with him.   Danger lies that way.

At the same time our love for God is the assurance of his love for us. In this it is different from all our poor human loves that it cannot fail of its return. In itself it unites us with its object. As long as you truly love God, you *cannot* be cut off from Him. That is pure illusion."

"But why, *why* should I feel cut off from him?"

"Didn't you say yourself that you never loved him more than now that you are cut off?"

"Yes," she whispered.

"Well, that's why. He seems to cut you off that you may desire him more; that you may draw nearer to him in work and prayer."

"Do you really think that?"

"I know it."

"Then I shall get back?"

"It may take time. Your trial may last weeks, months, years perhaps. But—you will get back."

"If I only could——"

"Only don't worry about getting back. Do God's will. Work. Work is the great cure. Go your old way, quietly working, and all will be well with you, dear Miss Lambert."

"I knew you would help me," she said.

"I'm very glad if I have helped you. But you will help yourself more. Work and pray.

Above all, work. We can't live forever on the spiritual heights, but our work is always near us."

"Yes, and it will be easy now that I know you are with me——"

She rose. He saw, not without misgiving that the look of exaltation had returned. He had brought it back.

"Of course, of course I am with you." He said it rapidly, perfunctorily, as a thing to which she must not attach too much weight.

When she had gone he meditated. It had been very dreadful. She had shown even more emotion than he had been prepared for, if he could say that he ever was prepared for emotion; it was a thing he couldn't get used to; each fresh exhibition of it gave him a fresh shock. But he had come through the ordeal wonderfully well, considering how he had dreaded it. The right words had been given him to say. That thought of his about our poor human loves was a particularly happy touch; it showed her very plainly that earthly love is apt to be a sad, frustrated affair and it referred her to the eternal consolation. And he was glad that he had remembered Spinoza. He was not only a priest, but a man handling a supremely difficult situation, and he felt that really he had acquitted himself very honourably.

As a priest he held himself ready to offer consolation; as a man he continued his austerities.

A week after this interview he came on Miss Lambert in Drayton Street where he was walking with Hilda Wrinch. He was aware of her a long way off, coming towards them on the other side of the road.

Miss Wrinch had pursued him through the market place, and caught him up at the bridge, and now insisted on walking with him down the street. She wanted to know what was going to be done about the Kempston Men's Club. The members were ceasing to turn up, the public houses were filling again, and the Club was coming to an end.

"I knew it wouldn't last," he said. "You cannot keep the men together."

"Billy Cartwright kept them together."

"Yes. But for how long?"

"As long as he was there. If he was there still it wouldn't have happened."

"Pardon me, it would have happened just the same. I know these village clubs. They catch on, run a few months and then drop, because everybody's tired of them."

"Because there's nobody to take an interest in them and keep them going. Mr. Fawcett doesn't even try."

"Mr. Fawcett knows too well what will succeed and what won't."

"Then aren't we to have any Men's Club in Queningford?"

"It's no use trying to after the Kempston experiment. If that had succeeded I shouldn't say——"

"It only wants somebody with Billy's energy to make it succeed. Why did you let him go?"

"I had no right to keep him."

"You talk as if he wanted to go. He didn't."

"He wanted to go where he would be most useful, Hilda. As for the Club, if a Club was wanted here we should have had one by now."

"What, with everybody sitting still and doing nothing?"

At this point Miss Lambert passed them. She went hurrying as if she were frightened, not smiling in return for his salute.

"I see," said Hilda. "None of poor Billy's plans are to be carried out."

"He was too full of plans for a small place like Queningford," he replied, and they parted.

About half past six in the afternoon of the

next day which was a Tuesday, one of the best days in the week for peace and comfort, he was sitting in his study, happily absorbed in a novel, when Pridget announced that Miss Lambert wished to see him and was in the drawing-room.

"Show Miss Lambert in here," he said, and Pridget showed her in.

Her face, strained by some dreadful purpose, foretold the destruction of his peace.

"Well," he said, "you wish to see me?"

"Yes. Last week I didn't tell you everything that was on my mind."

"Didn't you? And how was that?"

"I was afraid."

"Don't be afraid. Is it some new trouble?"

"No. It's nothing new. I have felt it for some time."

She paused.

"Come," he said, "tell me."

"I have felt that somehow I have offended you."

"Offended me? How could you possibly offend me?"

"That's it. I cannot think how. And yet I'm certain. Everything has been different lately."

(Ah, now it was coming. Last week would be nothing to the next half hour.)

"I feel—I feel that you are no longer with me as you used to be."

"There," he said, "you are utterly mistaken. What have I done or left undone that you should feel this?"

"Nothing. Nothing. It may be only in my own mind. And there is always what I spoke to you about the other day—that awful sense of being cut off."

"Patience. That will pass."

"Meanwhile I seem to have failed even in my work. There have been moments when I have felt that I could not go on. That it would be better for me to give it up."

"Give up your work?"

The idea terrified him. At any risk he must turn her from that disastrous course.

"Yes, to somebody younger and more energetic."

"Is it too much for you, then?"

"No. Not for my physical strength. But I feel all wrong. I seem to have lost hold."

"That, my dear Miss Lambert, is simply depression. It is part of the trouble you spoke of."

"No. It is that I think you are not satisfied with me. I feel as if I had lost touch with you completely in the last few months."

"I am more than satisfied. You have been my right hand ever since I came into this parish. You have relieved me of the whole material burden and given me leisure for spiritual things. I do not know what I should have done without you."

"Do you really mean that?"

"Of course I mean it. Have I ever said anything to make you doubt it?"

"No, you have said nothing."

"I've said nothing when I ought to have said a great deal. Well, I've said it now, and you believe me?"

"Yes, I believe you. You wouldn't tell me an untruth."

"And you won't talk about giving up your work?"

"Not if you really wish me to keep on."

"I wish you to keep on for your own sake as well as mine. I told you the other day that work was your salvation."

"I know it is. That was why I was so distressed to think that perhaps I ought to give it up. Nothing would distress me more."

Oh, he was sure of her.

"And now, let us see. You say you feel as if you had lost touch with me. I don't want you to feel that. Was it by any chance because of the change we made?"

"I think, perhaps, that may have had something to do with it. I do think we did work together better on the old plan."

"Well, then, let us return to the old plan. You will come and report to me once a week."

"If it isn't taking too much of your time."

"My dear lady, what is my time for? My time is my parishioners' time."

"You do understand?" she said. (Oh, she was innocent.) "Our weekly meetings were such a stimulus, such an encouragement."

"Well. Well, I am very glad to hear it."

Loud through the house the dressing bell clanged. It was half-past seven. Miss Lambert rose.

"Thank you," she said. "I knew you wouldn't fail me."

After she left him he meditated again.

Surely he had done well. Anything was better than letting her give up her work; better, incomparably better, than having to turn to and do it himself. And if seeing him weekly instead of monthly was the condition of her going on with it, then see her weekly he must and would. His peace and comfort were cheap at the price.

Considering peace and comfort only, it would be more endurable than these irregular upheavals which were the probable alternative.

As for what Charlotte had said, since the dear lady was very far from suspecting what was the matter with her, there was less danger for her in this moderate communion than in any rupture. Rupture might have enlightened her. The thing, the decent, sensible thing, was to go on as if nothing was the matter with her. Give her at least the benefit of her own innocence.

Anyhow, whatever happened, he couldn't do without her help. It saved him the expense of an additional curate, it enabled him to keep a butler and a head gardener, best of all, it secured for him the long leisure that he loved.

He sat down, well content, to a dinner of fried sole, roast pheasant, coffee cream, cheese soufflé, and a half bottle of sauterne.

CHAPTER XIV

IT was a cold, unpleasant day in the middle of January, too cold and unpleasant in the morning for the Rector to go out, too damp in the afternoon. He settled down in his arm-chair in the study, before a blazing fire, with a detective story. His mind, gently stimulated, followed with interest all the turns and windings of the plot; so ingenious was that plot, that of five possible murderers he had no idea which was the one who had killed Sir Godfrey. He had his theory, but as the work was obviously planned for the confounding of theories, he didn't really trust it. At intervals he crossed and uncrossed his legs as the heat of the fire stung them; time was measured for him by the moments when his right shin roasted and the moments of cooling in between. And when he was tired of crossing and uncrossing his legs he raised them, resting his feet on the chimney-piece, till the calves and the backs of his thighs were roasted, when he lowered them again. And while his legs endured the pleasant sting of the roasting his stomach was at peace, stretched out under an agreeable even warmth. He had also the resource of pushing his chair back from the fire and drawing it in again. After lunch he dozed. It was at three o'clock that the summons came: a note from Hilda Wrinch: Would he go to Duddington Farm at once and see old Mrs. Tombs who was dying?

Would he? The question as put by Hilda was hardly worth serious consideration. Yet he considered it. Would he go up to Duddington at once—*at once*—and see old Mrs. Tombs who was dying? Mrs. Tombs had been dying for some months, to his certain knowledge, and might remain dying for as many months more. And Duddington was five miles away, on the extreme northwestern limit of the parish. And it was going to rain. It might come down any minute. He sent round to the King's Head to ask if he could have the closed car. The car had gone into Cirencester and would not be back till the evening. That settled it. It was not a day to go driving about the country, sitting in an open tub of a governess cart; even if he took Scarrott and an umbrella.

No. He would not go at once.

But he would go. He would go first thing tomorrow morning.

And he settled again to his story. His whole mind was set, excitedly, on knowing which of the five had murdered Sir Godfrey.

At tea-time he ordered some good strong soup for Mrs. Tombs. He would take it to her in the morning. Another reason for putting off the visit; if he went now there would be no soup for Mrs. Tombs; soup to Mrs. Tombs was more than the consolations of religion, and Fuller's soup was better and stronger than any that could be made at the Farm. The thought of taking soup to Mrs. Tombs made him feel kind and benevolent; it worked in with the hot fire and his tea and his dinner to complete his outfit of agreeable sensations.

It was the girl who had murdered Sir Godfrey. He hadn't thought of the girl. He snuggled closer into his chair and began another detective story. That lasted him till ten o'clock, and at ten he went to bed.

The wind had got up in the night and rain was falling in thick sheets, dark in the dark. Every now and then the wind drove a sheet smack against his window pane. Rolled in three blankets and an eiderdown, with a rubber hot

water bottle cherishing his feet, he was exquisitely warm and comfortable. After the first turn
under the blankets he slid, by degrees of deeper
and deeper and more and more delicious drowsiness, into a perfect sleep. He dreamed that he
was starting on a railway journey for which it
was necessary that he should wear his surplice.
Hours passed while he looked for his surplice in
the vestry and the pulpit and his bathroom and
could find nothing but dinner napkins. He was
conscious of the train waiting for him in a black
station, while he opened an infinite series of
dressing table drawers. A bell rang somewhere
in a subterraneau place. He was waked by the
loud tapping of the rain on his window.

Was it the rain? Wasn't it too loud and sharp
and hard? He could hear the rain making a
noise of its own, a swishing noise, and the
shower of raps came pick-picking through the
swish. It was somebody throwing gravel up.

Somebody shouted, "Hallo, Canon Chamberlain! Hallo!"

A high, clear voice. He thought he knew it.

He got up, put on his dressing-gown, opened
the window and looked out. Down there in the
drive the light of two round lamps shone on the
wet hide of a pony and the front of a governess

cart, drawn up before the porch. It lit up (but imperfectly) the figure of a woman who stood under his window.

"Who's there?" he shouted.

"Hilda—Hilda Wrinch."

"What are you doing there?"

"I'm shouting to you to come down. I rang and couldn't make anybody hear."

"What's the matter?"

"Mrs. Tombs is dying."

At that he cried out in a lamentable voice, "I can't stay here at the open window."

"Don't," she shouted. "Come down and let me in. It's jolly wet out here."

"Wait a minute then."

With sharp, jerky movements that expressed his intense annoyance he dragged on his coat and trousers and went down. He turned on the light in the hall and opened the door to her.

In the stream of light he saw the figure of another woman huddled in the governess cart under an umbrella. Hilda came in. She had on her motoring coat and breeches, the rain poured from her hat on to the floor.

"Come into the study," he said, "it'll be warmer there."

In the study the remains of his great fire were

still burning. He drew up a chair for her. But Hilda remained standing. "We mustn't stay," she said, "we must be off at once."

He had not seized the implication of the plural, he supposed that it referred to the figure in the governess cart.

"Now, my dear Hilda, what *have* you come for at this unearthly hour?"

"I've come," she said, "to take you to Duddington."

"But—I haven't the remotest intention of going to Duddington tonight."

"You're going," she said grimly, "all the same. Why couldn't you go this afternoon? I *told* you Mrs. Tombs was dying."

"Mrs. Tombs," he said, "is always dying."

"Yes, but she's *really* doing it this time. She'll be dead if you don't hurry up."

"I don't suppose for a moment she'll be dead. I'm going over first thing in the morning. I was only waiting till I could have some soup to take to her."

"Soup? She's past soup, I tell you. Do hurry up and come."

"My dear girl, it's most unreasonable to expect me to turn out, straight out of bed, at this time of night and in all that rain."

"I'm out in it," said Hilda, "I've been out in it all day."

"Yes, my dear, but *you* hadn't gone to bed. If I could be of any use to Mrs. Tombs——"

"You can. She wants you."

"What for?"

"There's something on her mind, something she's done, I think. She's afraid of going to hell for it. You *must* come. You simply can't let the poor woman die in all that funk."

"Have you any idea what it is?"

He had a strong suspicion that Hilda had put it into Mrs. Tombs's head to send for him.

"Yes. I think it's something to do with Polly."

"Polly——?"

"Her daughter."

He remembered. Polly Tombs was the prostitute who lived in the slum off Drayton Street and danced on the table at the Three Magpies.

"I've got Polly there, in my cart."

"How did you get her?"

"I went and fetched her."

"You went—into *that* house?"

"Of course. You ought to be grateful to me for not leaving that job to *you*. I thought it would be rather worse for you than me."

"My dear——" He was shocked out of his sense of her unreasonableness. She had a nerve, this terrible young girl.

"It *was* pretty awful. Polly was in bed—like you. And I'd a frightful job to get her out of it. Business hours, you know. I had to stand and shout at the door for ever so long. And when she came out she was so drunk she could hardly stand.

"Is she—drunk—now?"

"Only half-drunk. She was sea-sick on the way and that's sobered her."

The prospect was more terrible than he could have conceived: to set out straight frim his warm bed in that open tub, to be shut up in it with the half-drunk and sea-sick Polly for a five-mile drive in the cold and the wind and the drenching rain, with the dreadful figure of Mrs. Tombs at the end of it. If he could have believed that she was really dying—but he had been "had" by Hilda so many times that he could not believe it. No: it was not reasonable to expect him to go through all that on the mere off-chance of Mrs. Tombs's dying. He stooped and built up the fire as if his position before it could be permanent.

"Never mind the fire," said Hilda. "Look

here, you mayn't like turning out in the rain any more than I do, but you've got to. You can't have it said that you were sent for to a dying woman and that you wouldn't go."

"I only want to be sure that she *is* dying."

"Then come and look at her. I'll swear to her dying, if that's all."

"You've been mistaken before now, Hilda ——"

"Oh damn! You've got to risk it."

"Yes. Yes. I suppose I have. Just wait till I've got some more things on."

"I say, you couldn't let me have an old overcoat, could you? I've had to lend Polly my British warm."

At last they started. He offered to drive, so as not to have to sit beside Polly Tombs, but Hilda wouldn't let him. He was not at all sure that she hadn't seen through his manœuvre, that she didn't take a fiendish pleasure in exposing him to the worst peril of the adventure. So he sat on the outside end of the cart, squeezed up beside Polly Tombs. Polly, wrapped in Hilda's British warm, was a large, inert mass that was shaken on to him and away from him by turns as the governess cart jolted, that made disagreeable noises, groaning and snuffling, and was wet with tears and rain. Rain from Polly's umbrella streamed down the back of his neck. Rain from the open sky beat on him; rain from the puddles on the road splashed up at him. The chilly wind rushed under the waterproof rug and shook it like a mad thing and blew up the corners; he had to keep pressing them down and pushing them under his own knees and Hilda's and Polly's. And always he had the fear of that horrible girl smiling—he was quite sure that Hilda was smiling—at his misery, and the more appalling fear of what might happen to Polly as the cart shook her. And he was seized with a great passion of longing for the warm, soft bed that he had left, and for the good sleep that had held him there, for the peace and safety of sleep.

They turned up a rough cart track through sodden fields; out of the dark and the wet there came the smell of swedes rotting in the rain. The farm-house loomed, lit by a light in an upper window. A poor place, barely more than a cottage.

They got out, Hilda led the pony under the shelter of a cart-shed, and they went into the house. A girl, the farm servant, came down the stairs with a lighted candle. An open doorway showed the lamp-lit kitchen at the back. Hilda left Polly there in the care of the servant and took the Rector up into the bedroom.

His fear of the horror to come increased with each step of the creaking, winding stair; and on the threshold of the room it met him. An acrid, pungent and sickening smell caught at his throat and choked him. The window of the room was closed and every chink in its frame was stuffed with newspaper; an old blanket hung before it above the cotton curtains. The heat of the fire and an oil lamp made the poison subtle and penetrating. He shut his mouth tight so as not to swallow it. His eyes turned, miserably, to the dying woman. She lay on a big high bed covered with soiled blankets, the end of the greyish sheet stretched tight across the mound of her waist. Her body, swollen with dropsy, was propped up with pillows; the yellowish skin, puffed taut and smooth like a bladder, had the look of wax and the smell of wax, mixed with something pungent, acrid and sickening.

He was still standing by the door.

He had never got over his terror of fœtid rooms, of the approach to the bedside. He knew that he ought to feel the pity, the solemnity, the poignancy of death; he could feel nothing but its poison and its squalor. He couldn't rise to

death's spiritual height; every time, he came to it
impotent and repugnant.

He saw Hilda going up to the bed, standing
close to the dreadful figure; she let the swollen
hand lie in hers, she stooped low over its face.
He wondered at her courage. She was trying
to hear what Mrs. Tombs was saying and to
make her hear.

"Canon Chamberlain has come to see you,"
she said, and signed to him to come closer. She
stood aside to let him take her place. He took it,
sickening. Hilda moved a chair up close beside
the bed. He drew it back a little and sat down.

"You'll have to go closer or she won't hear
you," she said.

Again he suspected her. She had perceived
his repulsion; she had let him in for the whole
ghastly business, and she took a malignant pleasure in holding him down to it, in seeing him go
through.

"Well, Mrs. Tombs, I'm sorry to hear you are
so ill," he began, and stuck. He couldn't, with
Hilda looking at him, he couldn't think what to
say next.

Mrs. Tombs moaned by way of answer.

"Ask her what she wants to speak to you
about," said Hilda.

"You have something to tell me, have you not? What is it?"

He could hear nothing but a sort of creaking in her throat and the words "something bad."

"Yes. What is it, Mrs. Tombs."

"Something bad I did." Her voice dropped, her breath came panting out at him, in gusts. He drew further back and saw Hilda look at him. He thought she smiled; but he wasn't sure, the flicker was so faint.

Mrs. Tombs's eyes wandered, looking for Hilda.

"*You* tell him, my dear," she whispered.

"Well, it's this. Mrs. Tombs is very unhappy because of something she did once."

"Something bad, say, my dear."

"Something bad."

"My—Polly——"

"Polly was away in a place. She got into trouble and had a baby, and Mrs. Tombs wouldn't let her come home. She shut the door on her when she came with the baby. And the baby died. And Polly took to bad ways."

"All along of me—shutting my door on her."

"She blames herself, you see. And she's afraid God won't forgive her for it. She thinks she won't get into heaven, because of Polly."

"I see. Well, Mrs. Tombs, you did a very wrong thing and a very cruel thing; but if you are sorry for it, if you truly repent and confess your sin before God, he will forgive you. You are sorry? You do truly repent?"

"Eh yes; but I'm sorry. All these weeks I've thought of nothing else, lying here. It's kept me awake, nights."

"Then, say after me: For what I did to my daughter Polly——"

"For what I did to my Polly——"

"I truly repent——"

"I truler repent——"

"And I confess my sin before God——"

"And I kerfess my sin before Gor——"

"Your sin is forgiven. If we confess our sins, God is faithful and just to forgive us our sins and to cleanse us from all unrighteousness. . . . I might read one or two of the Prayers for the Visitation of the Sick."

"If you think she's well enough."

"She seems to be well enough."

She seemed to him, in fact, not to be dying at all; at any rate she was no more dying than she had been a month ago. Hilda had brought him there, as usual, under false pretences. He knew that Hilda would be embarrassed and made uncomfortable by joining in the prayers for the Visitation of the Sick, and he was determined that she should join in them, that she should have a taste of the embarrassment and discomfort she had let him in for.

He hated having to pray aloud in that appalling air; still, it was his duty; he must go through with it. But as it was clear that Mrs. Tombs was in no state to take part in the responses, he contented himself with the Lord's Prayer and the prayer of Absolution.

"Our Lord Jesus Christ who hath left power to his Church to absolve all sinners who truly repent and believe in him, of his great mercy forgive thee thine offences: And by his authority committed to me, I absolve thee from all thy sins, In the Name of the Father, and of the Son and of the Holy Ghost. Amen."

Before the Lord's Prayer was finished Mrs. Tombs had fallen into a doze and remained unconscious of her absolution.

The Rector was pronouncing the Benediction when the door opened and Polly Tombs came in. Polly was crying quietly, but at the sight of her mother, a wave of hysteria swept her and she burst into loud, gulping, strangling grief. Hilda dealt with her.

"Stop that, Polly. You'll upset your mother. You can't stay with her, you know, if you won't keep quiet."

Polly was sober now; she gave one supreme sob and stopped.

"Polly's come to see you, Mrs. Tombs," said Hilda. She whispered to Polly, "Tell her you forgive her."

Polly stood staring at her mother. The wave of hysteria had returned and she began to cry again, though less noisily. Hilda led her to the bedside; and the Rector gave up his chair, retreating before the dreaded scene of emotion. And in a minute or two Hilda had followed him.

In silence they got into the governess cart and in silence they drove back in the cold, the darkness and the rain. As they turned into the Rectory drive, Hilda spoke.

"Aren't you glad I fetched you?"

"Glad? I don't think it was necessary," he said. "I might just as well have gone over in the morning. Mrs. Tombs isn't going to die to-night."

"You couldn't tell," said Hilda. "You couldn't possibly tell."

Mrs. Tombs did not die that night. In fact, she lingered for another ten days. For ten days, whenever he thought of Mrs. Tombs, the Rector had a queer, uncontrollable feeling of resentment. She hadn't played fair. He had turned out of his warm bed to give her peace in dying and the least she could have done was to have died.

He made Fawcett come over from Kempston Maisey to take Mrs. Tombs's funeral.

CHAPTER XV

THE following Sunday he preached on the subject of Peace; the peace which passeth all understanding. He spoke of the peace enjoyed by the saints and the mystics and all devout souls who have lived in close communion with God. He said that this peace, this communion was possible to all who truly seek it. He advised the practice of meditation, of thought fixed steadily on God or some attribute of God, his power, his goodness, his mercy, his love. A certain discipline of the mind was necessary. Meditation was the best means of overcoming that laziness of mind which was one of the most serious hindrances to the spiritual life. The spiritual life was not possible without frequent meditation upon God. It should be the prelude to all prayer. In meditation and the rest that comes after it the spirit recovers from its fatigue and receives new powers, just as the body recovers and receives new energy through sleep. And as in sleep we enter into a life in which bodily conditions are in a measure transcended, so in meditation we enter into a truly supernatural life. This life, he repeated, is not the special privilege of the few, but is open to everybody who will go through the discipline necessary to its attainment. He had got it all out of a little book published that month, a little book called *Mystic Experience* which a friend at Oxford had sent him as "one of the most spiritually illuminating things which have been written in our time."

The next morning he received a letter from Miss Lambert:

"My dear Canon Chamberlain:

"Thank you—*thank* you—for last night's sermon. I felt as if every word in it had been meant for me; it came as so complete an answer to the questions which have been troubling me lately. I wonder if you could tell me what books I could read on this subject—if you could lend me any? I feel that there is so much to learn and I cannot rest till I have learnt it. I have nothing but my Thomas à Kempis, which I know by heart.

"Perhaps you will tell me when I see you on Friday?

Very sincerely yrs.,

Agnes Lambert."

He waited till Friday. That gave him time to send to the London Library for the works of St. Teresa, St. John of the Cross and Julian of Norwich, which the author of *Mystic Experience* referred to frequently. It even gave him time to dip into the books, so that when Miss Lambert came to him on Friday he was able to say some very intelligent things about a subject of which otherwise he would have had to admit lamentable ignorance. All Wednesday, all Thursday and on Friday morning he soaked himself as well as he could in the *Life of St. Teresa by Herself,* in *The Dark Night of the Soul* and in the *Revelations of Divine Love.* Certain passages struck him. From St. John of the Cross.

"In this dark and arid night this blessed soul grows in the fear of God, and anxiety to serve him. For, as the breasts of sensuality, wherewith she fed and cherished the appetites whose lures she followed, are gradually withered up, her longing to serve God alone remains fixed, stubborn and naked, which is a thing most pleasing in his sight." . . . "But what this grief-stricken soul feels most of all, is the thought that God has most certainly forsaken her, and that in His loathing of her, He has cast her into the abyss of darkness, which is, for her, a grievous and pitiable suffering to believe that God has forsaken her." . . . "Profound and vast is this battle and combat, since the peace that awaits her shall be most deep; and spiritual grief is internal and rarified and searching, because the love she shall in time possess, must also be most internal and searching. . . . " "For on this road to descend is to mount and to mount is to descend."

From Julian of Norwich: "I saw that He is to us everything that is good and comfortable for us: He is our clothing that for love wrappeth us, claspeth us and all-encloseth us for tender love, that He may never leave us; being to us allthing that is good." . . . "till I am Substantially oned to Him, I may never have full rest nor very bliss . . . till I be so fastened to Him that there is right nought that is made betwixt my God and me." . . . "For our natural Will is to have God, and the Good Will of God is to have us; and we may never cease from willing nor from longing till we have Him in fullness of joy; and then we may no more desire."

He marked these passages for Miss Lambert.

His intelligence, which was the least lazy part of him, acknowledged that here was a wonderful life, wonderfully recorded; a life of such emotion, of such passion as he had not yet conceived; mysterious, incredible as it seemed, it so transcended all imagination that he was compelled to believe in its reality. At the same time, like all emotion, all passion, all mystery, like the spectacle of sickness and of dying, it made him feel profoundly uncomfortable. These books were for Miss Lambert, not for him.

She had stayed on after their usual discussion, shyly expectant.

"I have not forgotten you," he said. "I have a little book here, which may be useful. *Mystic Experience,* by a modern writer. It is, I think, one of the most spiritually illuminating things which has been written in our time." He did not add that it had bored him.

She murmured her thanks.

"And after that you might go on to the works of the great mystics themselves. I have sent for these books for you: the *Life of St. Teresa by Herself, The Dark Night of the Soul* by St. John of the Cross, and *Revelations of Divine Love* by Julian of Norwich. Here you will find the actual experiences recorded and will be able to compare them with your own."

"I ought not to speak about my own. I have had none. None but that deep consciousness of the presence of God, that sense of union with him."

"What more could you have?"

"I know there is something more. Do you really think, Canon Chamberlain, that the highest spiritual experience is possible for everybody?"

"I—I—the author of *Mystic Experience* says it is. He says 'there is no experience so high that the devout and disciplined soul may not attain to it.' But the soul must be devout, it must be disciplined. There is one way, the same for everybody. St. Teresa will show you the successive steps. And the end is one. Mystic experience, you will find, is one and the same all the world over. The same preparation, the same progress, the same goal. The mystic psychology is the same. You will see that no matter how great a genius the saint may be—and St. Teresa, St. John and Julian had genius—they are describing your states of soul as well as their own. The chief help of this reading will be to show you that where you thought you were alone you have great companions."

"The loneliness," she said, "has been awful."

"Well—in all your reading there are two things you must remember. First, that our Lord is the greatest companion, the supreme mystic.

Next, that the goal of the mystic way is not contemplation, it is not even union with God, but what has been called the unitive life. Union, I take it, is only the last stage but one. The highest is the life of *work*, of active service."

"You have always told me that. I have tried to live it."

"You have indeed. I know no one who has so well succeeded."

"I should have failed if you had not been here to keep me up."

"Not I," he said solemnly. "Not I, dear Miss Lambert."

"Sometimes one needs human help to keep near to God."

"Ah, yes." His voice sounded vague and inattentive. And he began piling up the four books.

"I will have these sent to your house."

But no. She insisted on carrying them herself, and she went off with *Mystic Experience*, St. John and Lady Julian in her satchel, and St. Teresa clasped to her heart.

He sighed as he watched her go. He was by this time aware that to get the best practical results out of Agnes Lambert he had to sustain her in her state of exaltation. Those books were the very thing. They would be fuel thrown to

her fire. Also he felt that in helping her to trans-
fer her affection from himself to God he would
be doing more for her than if he had returned it.
He saw her, simple, innocent, helpless as a clois-
tered nun, coming to him to report the progress
of her affair, babbling confidences. It was not
his duty to return Agnes Lambert's affection,
but it was his duty, his sacred duty, to let himself
be confided in. She looked to him in her help-
lessness to keep her mind fixed on the Eternal
Object of desire. He knew that once he had
given her the assurance of ultimate fulfilment,
she would come to him again and again, like a
love-sick girl, for that comfort. And in this way
he would strengthen his hold on her, securing
for himself the continuance of her devotion. He
had only to sit in his arm-chair, and listen, and
give her a little sympathy, once a week. He must
keep his hold.

The next Friday she said nothing but that she
was deep in the wonderful books he had lent her.
Two weeks passed before she again gave an account of her state.

"You were right," she said. "It has come back,
the peace and the happiness and that wonderful
sense of God's presence, of being one with him.
These books have helped me to get back. They

have shown me that that life is a reality; that it is the most real thing there is."

He asked her what she thought of St. Teresa.

"Oh, I felt as if she had written my life as well as her own. It was startling to come upon my own thoughts, my own feelings, to know there was nothing I had felt that she did not feel too. It's all there, all that terrible experience of being cut off, not able to get back. And that wonderful St. John of the Cross."

"Yes. It's what the saints call dryness. They all went through it. It seems to be part of the mystic experience."

"It does. And that has comforted me so much. I said to myself: If these great saints have had to go through with it, why not I? If they have come through into peace, into that wonderful blessedness, why not I?"

"Why not, indeed? I hoped you would feel that."

"Only—they had something more. That ecstacy, that actual vision of God. I cannot say I've had it. I'm afraid I never shall have it. Do you think it is possible—that highest state?"

"I—I can't say. How do you know that you are not in the highest state now, the state of work, of active service?"

"Because it goes in stages. One leads to the other. And I've missed the stage of ecstacy. If only I could get there. Then I should know. If I only had it once. If it never came again, I should know."

"Wait," he said: "wait. Who knows when it may come to you."

"The strange thing is that sometimes you feel it coming. You're on the edge of it. You feel as if something were going to happen. Only it never does."

He said again. "Wait."

"Yes. I must wait. I shall never be satisfied till I get there. The saints themselves were not satisfied with less."

"My own belief is that you have had it without knowing that you had it, and that you are now in the unitive life. The life's the thing. And so long as I see you living it, dear Miss Lambert, I can only believe that you have attained. But supposing you are never to be satisfied, say to yourself that this frustration is a necessary discipline, given to you to keep you humble."

"I've thought of that. I know I must accept whatever is sent me. And perhaps I am not disciplined enough. Perhaps, during Lent, with fasting and more prayer I may get nearer."

"Perhaps you may. The saints fasted and prayed. It isn't likely, is it? that we should attain with less effort, less discipline than theirs?"

"So long as you don't discourage me."

"Who am I that I should discourage you?"

"Oh, you——" And it was as if she said, How shall I find words to say what you are?

And so there began for Agnes Lambert a life of certain and increasing exaltation. Her soul soared higher and higher in its spiral round of prayer and meditation. She lived on the very edge of ecstasy. She perfected her spiritual technique; she learned the method of self-emptying, the unique surrender. She made darkness round her, darkness in which all thought, all feeling, all sensation died. She waited for God to fill her emptiness; in her darkness she waited for the light. She made a practice of sitting in the church before twilight, for meditation. There, with her eyes fixed on the shining cross above the altar, she imagined her life flowing from her, flowing, flowing, into the life of God; she imagined the life of God flowing out and out from him into her; the two tides met and mingled. And always in the line of her divine vision and across it, the imagined figure of Clement Chamberlain stood behind the altar rail, in surplice and stole.

She saw his hand lifted in the Benediction and heard his voice saying: "The peace of God, which passeth all understanding, keep your hearts and minds in the knowledge and love of God and of his Son Jesus Christ our Lord; and the blessing of God Almighty, the Father, the Son, and the Holy Ghost, be amongst you and remain with you always."

And so far from this image interfering with her approaching ecstasy, it seemed to help it, to draw out her soul towards itself and away, behind the altar, behind the cross, behind the great east window painted with the Crucifixion, out to the infinite Reality beyond.

And with Lent came more meditation, more prayer, and fasting.

CHAPTER XVI

IT was in Mid-Lent that Dr. Lawson called at the Rectory. He was shown into the study where he found Canon Chamberlain absorbed, happily, in a volume of *Reminiscences*. The Rector was extraordinarily bland and benevolent, for he thought that Dr. Lawson had come as usual to recommend some candidate for soup, and the thought of giving away soup always made him benevolent and bland.

"What can I do for you today, Lawson?" he said, implying that there was no day on which he was not prepared to do something for the doctor. "Soup?"

"No. It isn't soup. I want to consult you about one of your parishioners. I daresay you know who I mean."

"I haven't a notion, unless it's Mary Curtis. She hasn't got another illegitimate baby, has she?"

Dr. Lawson smiled. "It isn't Mary Curtis. It's Agnes Lambert."

"Agnes Lambert? You don't mean to tell me *she's* ill. She was perfectly well last Friday."

"She's anything but perfectly well. She'll be very ill indeed, Canon Chamberlain, if you don't take care."

"If *I* don't take care? What on earth have *I* got to do with Agnes Lambert's illness—if she is ill?"

"A good deal more than you think. She is in a very dangerous state."

"What sort of state?"

"Well—a state of unnatural exaltation."

"Unnatural?"

"I mean what I say."

"It depends on the nature. What may seem unnatural to you, Lawson, may be perfectly natural to Agnes Lambert—or to me. Agnes Lambert is a born mystic."

"She's a made fanatic, if that's what you mean. And if you don't take precious good care she'll be a borderland case before she's done. She's on the verge of religious mania now."

The Rector was unperturbed.

"Nothing of the sort. I know all about Miss Lambert's spiritual state. I've had the direction of it for seven months.

"You have? Then I suppose you're aware that

she goes about saying that she expects shortly to be united with the Deity?"

"She told *you* that?"

"No. She told Mrs. Fawcett who told my wife. Also, she's gone in for fasting, with a view, I suppose, to hastening the happy consummation. And I gather that you approve of all this."

"Certainly I approve. Fasting in Lent is not unusual among religious people. As for Miss Lambert's religious ideas, I must decline to discuss them with you."

"Why not? It's precisely those ideas that I want to discuss."

"It's useless to discuss what you don't understand."

"I understand perfectly."

"Pardon me, every word you've uttered shows that you do not. You evidently put the most gross and material construction on the most spiritual things."

"Oh, of course if you encourage her in thinking that she's spiritual, it's hopeless."

"She is spiritual. Deeply spiritual. That is why nothing you can say, Lawson, is the least likely to apply. You must allow me to understand her case better than you do."

"I doubt if you understand her physical condition. You must allow me to be the best judge of that. Fasting is simply suicide. At least it's madness. I mean literally madness. Seriously, she's on the edge of a bad nervous breakdown. She's had one before, a slight one, at Southwark. That's why she had to leave."

"I didn't know that."

"You know now. And when you get abnormal ideas working on an unbalanced and ill-nourished brain, what can you expect?"

"If fasting is bad for her it shall be discontinued. But I deny that her ideas are abnormal. They are the ideas that every saint and mystic has had all the world over."

"Saints and mystics, all the world over, have been thoroughly abnormal people."

"Oh, no, Lawson; they only seem so to you because you haven't a notion of what mysticism really is. There's no doubt that Agnes Lambert has had moments of religious depression. She must have been suffering in this way when she left Southwark. But I've succeeded in persuading her that this state is illusory, and that it will pass. It *has* passed, and she is happy again. And as long as she is happy and at peace I have no fear for her."

"Well, I *have*. I *know* that it's when she's what you call happy and at peace that she's in the greatest danger. Her only chance is to get away from Queningford."

"From Queningford? Where she's happy, where she has work and friends?"

"I tell you the happiness and the work are all part of it. They help to keep up the delusion. As for her friends, I can't see what good they've been to her."

"No, you can't see. You can't see. That's what's wrong with you, Lawson."

"I see well enough that she'll go off her head if she stays here another three months."

"Where can she go to?"

"There's a sister at Bournemouth who'd give her a home."

"You've written to this sister?"

"Yes. She agrees with me."

"That doesn't sound as if Miss Lambert would be very happy with her sister."

"I believe they're extremely fond of each other. She's quite prepared to go, only she says she must talk to you about it first."

"That's only natural."

"Yes. Only too natural. I believe she means to ask your advice and abide by it. And she *will* abide by it. Nobody has any influence with her but you."

Canon Chamberlain neither admitted nor denied it; he looked urbanely capable of anything.

"I do beg of you, Canon, not to advise her to stay."

"I shall advise her to the very best of my ability, you may be sure."

"If I were sure that you realised your responsibility."

"I do realise it. But I must look at the case all round."

"I don't know what looking at it all round means. But I do know that if you keep her here you'll be letting her in for the very gravest risk."

"I shall consider that risk, among other things."

But what the other things were that he would consider he did not say. It was clear that the doctor had no confidence in him.

"Whatever you do," he said, "for Goodness' sake don't encourage her in this idea she's got about God."

The Rector's answer was a strange, mysterious smile, the smile of an understanding that had not been vouchsafed to Lawson. It made the doctor feel more uneasy than ever.

"Well," he said, "I only wish I had half your influence," and went.

After he was gone the Rector sat for some time with his elbows comfortably supported on the arms of his chair, and his hands raised to his chin, joined palm to palm and finger-tip to finger-tip. It was the attitude of prayer. But the Rector was not praying, he was thinking hard.

Presently he turned to his *Reminiscences*.

The next day which was a Tuesday, after twilight had come, Miss Lambert called. She begged that the lamp might not be lit and that they might sit in the twilight. She said it was so peaceful. But it was clear that she took refuge in the dusk to hide her agitation. Her voice quivered.

"I've come to ask your advice," she said.

"You shall have the best I can give you."

"I believe Dr. Lawson saw you yesterday."

"He did."

"And he told you I was ill, or that I should be ill if I did not take care."

"He seemed to think so. We agreed that this fasting might not be good for you, and I promised him that it should be given up."

"That was not all."

"No. That was not all. He thinks you are suffering from over-strain."

"Over-strain. That's what he says it is. He thinks I ought to go away. Right away."

"Ah, yes. He did say something."

"I told him I shouldn't dream of taking such a step without consulting you."

"Quite right."

"He says my work isn't good for me and that I'm living in a narrow round of monotonous ideas, and that I ought to be shaken out of myself. He wants me to go and live with my sister."

"Would you like to live with your sister?"

"Yes, if she lived in Queningford. But I cannot bear, no, I can *not* bear to leave dear Queningford. I love every man, woman and child in it; I love every house, every tree and stone. I should be lost if I left it."

"You should, perhaps, have less to do."

"No. No. It isn't my work. Even Dr. Lawson doesn't say it is. My work is what keeps me well. It's what he calls my narrow round of ideas."

"He *would* call it narrow."

"Yes. He doesn't know. But you know. You understand. The ideas he calls narrow are wider than the world; they are the way out from narrowness; they are reality to you and me."

He made a gesture of assent.

"I'm afraid we shall never get him to see it. I had a long talk with him yesterday and it was quite clear to me that he doesn't see. He's a case of scientific blindness."

"If I were to do as he tells me, I should give up the whole practice of religion. Give up everything that makes my life and my happiness."

"It's preposterous."

"Isn't it?"

"Your mind is too fine to be dragged down to his level."

"How am I to make him understand the happiness and peace that have come to me in the last three weeks?"

"You couldn't. He's incapable of understanding such a thing as mystical experience. It's abnormal to him, and I might talk till Doomsday before I could convince him that for certain people it's the only normal state. As for giving up religious practices, your peace and happiness are the best assurance you could have that they are necessary and they are right."

"Perhaps it was foolish of me to speak of mystic experience to Mrs. Fawcett. But she saw

232

the book lying on my table and asked what it was, and I tried to tell her."

"Better not. Better not. Let her read for herself and you keep your own secret."

"That's it. Have I any right to keep it to myself when it might bring happiness to some other person?"

"I think you have the right when you know that the other person will not understand; will only go away with some gross idea. You are keeping nothing from her. The same means of grace are open to everybody. I am not sure, after seeing Lawson, that mystic experience *is* for all of us."

"I can't bear to think of dear Dr. Lawson being shut out."

"He isn't shut out. He shuts himself out."

"You wouldn't be frightened, then, if you were me?"

"Frightened? He hasn't been frightening you, has he?"

"Well, just a little. He did seem to think I was in a very morbid state."

"It's he who's in a morbid state. No. There is nothing to be afraid of. You are safe. Absolutely safe. Would that all my parishioners were as sound and sane."

"And—am I to go or stay?"

"Stay. Stay, dear Miss Lambert, as long as you are happy with us, and happy in your work. Haven't I told you that I can't do without you?"

She looked at him. A long look of joy and satisfaction. Her face was lit up, her eyes shimmered as if through tears: light of blessedness, shimmer of ecstacy.

CHAPTER XVII

WHEN Mrs. Hancock's cousin, Mrs. Beauchamp, took Queningford House everybody was excited.

She was preceded by rumours of her widowhood, her wealth, her large staff of servants, her Rolls-Royce car and her chauffeur; of the expensive improvements she had made in Queningford House.

Everybody wanted to see what the improvements were, and what the rich widow was like. Everybody called. The Rector was one of the first.

The evidences of wealth met him as he entered. By sacrificing the morning room Mrs. Beauchamp had turned the hall into a long, wide lounge, and she had thrown out a wing into the garden on the south to replace the morning room. She had panelled the lounge with old oak and put in an old oak staircase to match. She had lengthened the drawing room by throwing out another wing to balance the new morning room, and she had made a flagged court, with flower beds set in it, between the wings.

He had time to observe these changes while he waited for her, sitting in an armchair so exquisitely comfortable that he could have wished to sit in it for hours together doing nothing, absorbed in the sense of rest. The whole house was hushed in a perfect stillness and peace. The very clock as it struck four had a soothing, droning note. It was Friday and he had to be back at the Rectory at half past four to meet Miss Lambert. The thought was very unpleasant. He was also torn between the hope that Mrs. Beauchamp might come in soon, so that he might get away soon, and his desire to be let alone, to remain in that blessed comfort, undisturbed.

Mrs. Beauchamp did not keep him waiting long.

A small, very plump and round, very white and soft woman. Little handsome nose and mouth in a plump round face, very white and soft like a full blown white rose. The pouting mouth and trumpeting cheeks of a cherub. Large eyes, rich and liquid and very dark. A mass of rich, sleek dark hair. Forty, not more, perhaps younger.

She moved with a noiseless, elastic, padded roll.

"How good of you to call——"

Her voice came deep and sweet out of her plumpness, with a musical vibration.

She settled herself on the sofa among the down cushions, plump to the plump, making a harmony of soft round curves.

He said he was delighted.

"I hoped you'd come soon. I've heard so much of you from Kitty Hancock."

"Mrs. Hancock is always good to me. She must be very glad to have you here."

"Yes, Kitty and I are great friends."

"And I'm sure," he went on, "that Queningford is very glad to have you."

"That's very nice of Queningford," she said, and he expressed the hope that she would like Queningford.

"Oh yes, dear Queningford. I fell in love with it at first sight. It looks such a happy, comfortable, peaceful place."

"It is. On the whole it is. Comfortable and peaceful. And I think you will find us a very happy little community."

She laughed a little cooing laugh that came up out of her breasts, shaking them under her thin black tunic. A happy laugh. He was beginning to like Mrs. Beauchamp.

"I'm afraid," she said, "I'm very fond of peace and comfort. *And* happiness."

"So am I. We shall agree, then."

"Kitty Hancock tells me you're very strict. You don't allow any back-biting or gossip. How do they manage to get on without it?"

"Oh, I don't know what goes on behind my back. I can only put my foot down when I'm there."

She laughed again.

"I'm afraid you'll have to put it down on me," she said, "I like people and I like talking about them."

"Oh, if you only talk because you like them, that's another thing."

"Still, it's gossip. I like to know what they do with themselves all day, and who's going to marry who, and what's the matter with them when they're ill."

He smiled indulgently. There was something about her that made him feel indulgent. He liked her because she liked peace and comfort.

"Only," she said. "There's one thing I may as well tell you at once. *Don't* ask me to do any parish work."

"I wasn't going to ask you."

"Nor," she said, "to talk about it. I can't take an interest in the parish. . . . I'm afraid you'll want me to take an interest."

"I shouldn't dream of boring you with the parish."

"It *would* bore me, horribly."

"Between ourselves, Mrs. Beauchamp, it bores me. Only you mustn't tell anybody I said so."

"Oh, does it? How nice of you to be bored, like me."

He laughed. She was naïve, and he liked her.

"But, of course, I'll subscribe to things. I'll take *that* sort of interest."

"It's very good of you."

"Oh no, it's the least one can do when one dumps oneself down on an innocent place. You'll come to me, won't you, when you want subscriptions?"

"I shall not forget your kind promise."

And the idea of subscriptions suggesting expenditure, he complimented her on the improvements she had made.

"I have got it nice and comfy, haven't I? There'll be sun all day long in my two wings. You see how the windows look south, east and west. I shall simply sit and soak in the sun."

She would, she would, like a soft, plump, comfortable cat. He thought he would like to see her doing it. For Mrs. Beauchamp's presence had a remarkable effect on him; so far from disturbing him, it doubled his sense of peace and comfort; warmth seemed to beat out of her.

The hand of the clock was moving towards the half hour. He thought of Miss Lambert with distaste. At that moment the parlour-maid came in, bringing the tea-things. There was a flutter of snow-white linen and the pleasant tinkle of china and of silver. And a smell of hot butter.

He rose.

"Oh, don't go just as tea's coming in. Please stay and have some."

"I should like to. I should like to of all things; but Miss Lambert will be waiting for me at the Rectory. I should be there by half-past."

"You'll be there by five and twenty to."

She had poured out his cup. He had a vision of small, delicate home-made scones, hot-buttered. Never in all his life had he been able to resist home-made scones, hot-buttered. He hesitated and stayed.

"You shall go," she said, "the very minute you've finished your tea."

"I'm afraid I shall have to be guilty of that unpardonable rudeness."

It was delicious, sitting there in the deep, soft-cushioned chair, eating hot buttered scones, drinking China tea with the smoky flavour that he loved, and watching the plump but dainty hands hovering about the tea-cups and the dishes. Mrs. Beauchamp enjoyed tea-time and was determined that he should enjoy it too.

The tea-cups (he noticed such things) were wide and shallow and had a pattern of light green and gold on white, with a broad green and gold band inside, under the brim. His nostrils drank in the fragrance.

"I wonder why it is," he said, "that a green lining to a cup makes tea so much more delicious. But it does."

"I know it does," she said with feeling.

"There's a house here where they give you strong Indian tea in dark-blue china. You can't imagine anything more horrible."

"It would be."

"And all tea-cups should be wide and shallow."

"Yes. It's like champagne in wide glasses, isn't it?"

"A larger surface for the scent, I suppose."

"Funny that there should be light green tastes

and dark blue tastes, but there are. Only I didn't think anybody noticed it but me."

Delightful community of sense. And like himself she felt that these things were serious.

He ate two scones, but refused, stoically, a second cup of tea, and tore himself away.

"What a pity," she said, "you had that appointment."

It *was* a pity. And he was exactly thirteen minutes late for it, too. In the Rectory drawing-room Miss Lambert waited, patient and resigned. He said that Mrs. Beauchamp had made it difficult for him to get away; which was true. And he hoped she would forgive him.

He called at Queningford House again and again; only never again on a Friday. He found that he could spend hours sitting in that perfect chair (Mrs. Beauchamp had advanced so far in friendliness as to put cushions at his back), drinking and eating, smoking his afternoon cigarette and talking to Mrs. Beauchamp about the simple matters that she loved; food and the people she had seen, and what she was going to do in her kitchen garden. She envied him his hothouse and his beautiful grapes. And did he know whether the Queningford House peach-trees bore well? He seemed to remember from last year peaches small but fine flavoured. She was going to enlarge the strawberry bed.

"You'll come and see me in the summer and we shall eat strawberries and cream out in the garden."

Charming. And she would come and eat *his* strawberries and *his* cream in the Rectory garden.

Occasionally he sent her grapes from his hothouse.

And he gave a succession of luncheon parties and tea parties and dinner parties for Mrs. Beauchamp, asking only what he called "the best people." Mrs. Beauchamp was worthy of the best. He liked entertaining her. He wanted her to see what Fuller could do. He knew that Fuller was celebrated as the best cook on that side of the county. They had nothing like her at the Manor, or Kempston Hall, or any of the big houses round about Queningford.

And then Mrs. Beauchamp asked him back again. To luncheon first. He had to admit that in that luncheon, Fuller, the otherwise incomparable Fuller, was surpassed. There never was such a luncheon. Never had he eaten, nay, never ordered, nor yet had he conceived such a luncheon. But dinner would be the test. Not till he

had dined with Mrs. Beauchamp would he own
that he was beaten.

He dined.

The dinner was better than the luncheon.
And Radford (Radford was the name of the
genius who had created it) Radford had out-
done herself in his honour.

"I told her you were coming," Mrs. Beauchamp said. "How is it that a cook will always
cook better for a man than a woman? Do you
know more, or care more, or both?"

He thought both. But he recognised her as the
great exception. She cared and knew.

Perhaps in London or New York, in the houses
of millionaires that dinner might have been
equalled; it could not have been surpassed. Radford excelled Fuller not only in sheer brilliance
of technique but in the richness and the range of
her imagination. She sent up dishes that he had
never seen nor remembered nor dreamed of; fan-
tasties, poems. In all her works there were har-
monies, linked sequences, progressions, cumula-
tive effects. A luncheon or a dinner was not a
mere succession of good dishes, it was a wonderful, concerted whole, it had significance, drama,
a beginning, middle and end.

And as he lunched and dined with Mrs. Beauchamp again and again he saw that this imagination of Radford's knew no bounds; with incredible versatility it threw off masterpiece after masterpiece, not two alike.

He thought of what life would be if only he had Radford.

Again and again the Rolls-Royce tore through the market place with a "honk" at the corner of London Street and a "honk" at the Rectory gate, and would return with the Rector in it, either alone or with Mrs. Beauchamp. For Mrs. Beauchamp had placed her car at his disposal. They were seen driving together in and out of Cirencester and miles beyond the bounds of the parish. It was even said that she had taken him to Oxford and back.

He knew that people were beginning to talk; but he didn't care; and it was evident that Mrs. Beauchamp didn't care either.

He thought of what life would be if only he could have that car and the chauffeur, Rendall.

He found this friendship with Mrs. Beauchamp entirely delightful. It was so easy to get on with her, so easy to talk to her. About anything. About the novels they had been reading; and the Reminiscences (she liked them mildly scandalous; another link); about food and gardens, and foreign travel, about the Riviera (she had been there and preferred Cap Martin to Cannes) and the Riviera hotels; about France and Germany and America and Turkey (she was always glad to listen to his views on the political situation, having none of her own; things, she said were getting much too complicated for her poor brain). They talked about people whom they knew. They talked about Kitty Hancock.

"She *has* been brave," said Molly Beauchamp. He knew now that her name was Molly. It suited her; a soft, plump name.

"Very brave," he said, and felt a twinge of compunction. It was weeks since he had called to see Kitty Hancock, months since he had thought of her. In moments of reverie it was not Kitty's slender black and ivory that he saw but something round and soft and plump, with a cherub's face that smiled at him with a cherub's mouth crushed between two blown cheeks, and eyes that were round and soft and had a kind of plumpness, too. A dewy plumpness. Molly.

"She *has* brought up those children well," said Molly.

"Come, aren't they a little too obstreperous?"

"Oh, they're scamps. But such darling scamps. Well, I don't suppose Kitty'll ever marry again."

"Why not?"

"Because of them. She isn't going to give those big boys a step-father; and he'd be a bold man who'd tackle the five of them."

"You think so?"

"Well, yes. Very few men would be content to come after the youngest of five children, just to take what was left of Kitty when they'd done with her. After Gerald's death, too."

"There wouldn't be very much left," he said. He was thinking that all of Molly had been left after her husband's death. Molly had no children. But of course you couldn't tell whether that was—— He knew that she had been her husband's second wife and he wondered whether *he* had had children. He wished he knew.

They were sitting in her drawing room and facing him on a side table was the photograph of a young man in uniform. He got up and looked at it, saying what a fine face it was.

"Yes. Isn't it a dear face? That's my stepson. My husband's youngest boy. His brother was killed at Vimy Ridge. And he's the last of them."

"Really?" he said. "How sad."

He knew what he wanted to know. And

still—— He wondered whether the boy lived with her.

"He looks young to be married, doesn't he?" she said.

And he thought what life would be like if only he could have Molly Beauchamp.

CHAPTER XVIII

QUENINGFORD HOUSE stands with its back turned north to the street and its living rooms facing the garden on the south. So that while everybody who goes to Queningford House can be observed from the windows of the house opposite, when he is once fairly inside the most inquisitive eyes cannot see what has become of him.

Miss Lambert's cottage was the house opposite. And from its windows she watched the Rector as he came and went. Two or three times a week he came and went. She counted the times. Every now and then as he stood on the doorstep he was aware of a vague form moving behind the window of the house opposite, and of a face at the pane. A form, a face, that drew back suddenly when he turned towards it. At other times it would be motionless, yet he knew that it was there, watching him. But he paid no attention. He was past paying attention to anything that was not Molly Beauchamp.

And sometimes, as she went from door to door in Queningford, Miss Lambert would hear the noise of a motor car, and the Rolls-Royce would rush past her, carrying Mrs. Beauchamp and the Rector, or sometimes, but not often, the Rector alone. From his attitude of happy ease she judged the extent of their intimacy. At the same time she refused to believe the evidence of her senses. She didn't want to believe it.

Then one day Miss Minchin came to see her. It was clear that she had come on purpose to say something, and she did not wait long before she had said it.

"Well, I suppose we shall soon be hearing of an engagement in Queningford."

"Whose engagement?"

"The Rector and Mrs. Beauchamp, of course."

Miss Lambert felt the little room beginning to rock and turn round. She gripped the edge of the table hard to give herself a sense of security. Miss Minchin kept her small, malicious eyes fixed on her.

"They're always together," she said. "He drives about with her all over the country, and they say he's never out of her house."

"It doesn't mean anything," Miss Lambert said.

"Oh, doesn't it? It can only mean one thing. I'm expecting every minute to hear that they're going to be married."

"It isn't in the least likely. The Rector isn't a marrying man; and Mrs. Beauchamp is not the sort of woman he'd care for, if he was."

"I should say she was very much the sort. Anyhow, my dear Agnes, you can't expect him to stay a bachelor forever, just to please you."

"I believe in the celibacy of the clergy. So does he."

"Well, it doesn't look as if he did."

And, her purpose accomplished, Miss Minchin kissed her dear Agnes, borrowed a book as a pretext, and went away.

That evening when Miss Lambert sat in the church to meditate, no meditation came. Lent was over, and Easter, Easter, this year, had brought her no joy. She had tried to feel uplifted by it, but she had not been uplifted, she had been depressed. She had received the Sacrament with no deep sense of having received it. And today she couldn't even meditate. She no longer felt her life flowing out from her into the life of God, and the life of God flowing into her, filling her, satisfying her, restoring her. Instead of thinking about God, she found herself thinking about nothing, nothing at all. And this was not the mystic self-emptying and self-surrender; it was nothing but nothing. And then, suddenly, before she could save herself, the images of Clement Chamberlain and Mrs. Beauchamp came rushing in. She saw them standing together before the altar rail, bridegroom and bride. She saw them driving away in the Rolls-Royce, afterwards. She had a vision of a large double bed in a hotel, Clement Chamberlain's face on one pillow and Mrs. Beauchamp's on the other. This vision was very solid and distinct. She could see the little fat mound Mrs. Beauchamp made under the bed-clothes. That frightened her. She was shocked at herself. And then she covered her face and her eyes with her hands to shut it all out, and tried to pray.

But she couldn't pray.

Then she began mechanically saying the General Confession, the Lord's Prayer and the Collect for the week, over and over again, rather fast, without thinking. She stayed a long while kneeling there, while the slow, clear April dusk gathered in the aisles and the windows darkened.

That night when she lay awake in her bed, under the crucifix, she tried to get back into her peace; but it was no use. She made darkness round her as before, but there was no peace in it and no sense of the presence of God. There was nothing. Nothing. She was more cut off than she had ever been. Her mind swam in the darkness, without thought, struggling to get through to God. She felt as if she were snared in a net, bound with iron; an iron weight was on her breast, pressing down her breath; she panted, turned and twisted, trying to shake off the weight. But the more she struggled the heavier it pressed on her. Suffocating her. It was unendurable. It was like death. She remembered then that St. Teresa and St. John of the Cross had gone through this state. They had described it. Saint Teresa had said: "it is like a person who having a rope round his neck tries to breathe." She had said of the God-tormented soul: "No consolation reaches it from heaven and it is not there itself; it wishes for none from earth and it is not there either, but it is, as it were, crucified between earth and heaven, enduring its passion."

That was it; the struggling, the fighting for breath, the crucifixion. This state that she was in was the Dark Night of the Soul, the real thing. She had a sudden longing to see again what St.

John of the Cross had said about it. She lit a candle and took up the book that lay on the little table at the head of her bed.

She read again of "the harsh and cruel purgation of the spirit." Ah, harsh and cruel, that was what it was. Harsh and cruel . . . "he strips them of the powers and affections and senses, spiritual as well as sensible, interior as well as exterior, leaving the mind in darkness, and the Will stranded, and the memory void, and the desires of the soul in profound distress, bitterness and conflict."

That had been done to her. The Will stranded and the memory void.

And again: "ofttimes she is overtaken by such absences of mind, such profound lapses of memory, that for long intervals together, she is unconscious of what she did or thought, or what she is doing or is about to do, nor can she concentrate her attention, in spite of all her efforts, on anything she is engaged upon."

That was her state. Her spirit, too, was "placed in intense anguish and conflict, and every friendly and pleasant impression banished from the memory, with the most profound sensation and interior conviction of having travelled far away from, and become a stranger to, all things, wherein it seems to her that all are foreign to her and changed from what they were.'

She read about the soul's redemption, passages that Clement Chamberlain had marked for her; she read mechanically, without any belief in what she read.

"Then, oh! Spiritual Soul, when thou shalt see thy inclination darkened, they affections withered up and crushed, and thy faculties disabled for all interior exercise, let it not grieve Thee, rather count it for great good fortune; for God is even now on the way to deliver thee from thyself, taking from thee thy possessions; wherewith, however willingly they helped thee, thou couldest not proceed so consummately, perfectly and safely . . . as now, when God takes thee by the hand and leads thee like a blind man through the darkness, whither and by what paths thou knowest not. . . ."

She had felt that once, too. But not now. Not now.

"After this fashion doth the soul go forth from herself and all created things to the sweet and delightful union of love of God, 'In darkness and in safety.'" . . .

"These souls" (the daring ones) "get from God what with delight they ask of him." . . .

"In this way, by this Mystical Theology and Secret Love, doth the soul go, going forth from all things and from herself, and mounting to God. . . . "

But not she. These words had no meaning for her. Nothing had meaning for her but the words that described her suffering.

"Wherefore he who shall refuse to set forth into this night . . . , to seek for his Beloved and be stripped of his will and mortified, but who seeks for Him in his bed and at his ease shall find him not. . . ."

Spiritual lust (St. John of the Cross had terrible phrases) and spiritual sloth together, was *that* her sin? If that was it, she would rise and seek God upright on her knees, on the cold, hard floor.

Yet what was the good of seeking, since for her this "dark and arid" night of the soul would never end? She would never rise up out of the darkness. She was cut off from God utterly and forever.

Through all her misery she was sustained by one thought. Tomorrow she would go and see Canon Chamberlain. He would tell her what to think; he would help her to bear it. It was not a Friday; it was, in fact, a Thursday, but she couldn't hold out another day. She longed for the comfort that he gave her.

She knew that he disliked being called on in the morning, therefore, with a great effort, she forced herself to wait till twenty minutes to four, and then she started for the Rectory.

She arrived punctually at ten minutes to four, the very moment when the Rector was in the hall, putting on his hat to go to Queningford House. He was feeling nervous and impatient, for after much consideration he had made up his mind that there was nothing in the world he wanted so much as to marry Mrs. Beauchamp. He was going to ask her to marry him that afternoon. If nothing happened to prevent him he would be doing it about five o'clock, or a little later, after tea. It would be all settled one way or another by then. He thought that by leaving before four o'clock he would avoid visitors to the Rectory and forestall Mrs. Beauchamp's visitors. And he would then ask to see her alone. And then—— And then——

As he went out he met Miss Lambert on his doorstep. He didn't know whether his face showed his shock of annoyance. He could feel himself pulling the stiff muscles of his mouth into some sort of a smile.

"Well, Miss Lambert, I'm afraid—I'm afraid I have to go out."

"If you could see me for one minute. I won't keep you longer."

"Won't it do tomorrow? I could see you then."

"No. Or I shouldn't have come today. Please, one minute."

"Well, come in, I'm afraid I can't spare *more* than one minute."

He thought of asking her to call again at six, but, besides disapproving of this discourtesy, he reflected that it would be better to see her at once and get it over. He would then be justified in cutting it very short. Better than tying himself up for an interminable interview later on when— when he might be no more in the mood for Miss Lambert than he was now.

He led the way into his study—he felt that his study constrained him less to a leisurely politeness than his drawing room. He made Miss Lambert sit in his armchair while he remained standing, to remind her that their communion must be brief.

"Well," he said, "what is it?"

"It's come back."

"What has come back?"

"That awful feeling."

"Oh——" His voice expressed no eagerness nor even interest.

"Only it's worse than ever. It's indescribable. I never felt more cut off than I feel now."

"It'll pass," he said. "It has passed. It will pass again."

"No. I know now that it will never pass."

"You've said that before. And yet——"

"Do you think," she said, "it *is* the dark night of the soul?"

"Do I think——? Really, Miss Lambert, I don't know what to think. You must know what it is better than I do."

It was four o'clock. If he couldn't get rid of her in five minutes he might be too late for Mrs. Beauchamp. Other visitors might get in before him.

"You told me," she said, "that it was that. What St. John of the Cross had."

He hadn't thought about St. John of the Cross from that day to this, and he had completely forgotten what he had told her. He didn't know, for the life of him, what to say to the poor thing. But he remembered that he had once known.

Ah—now it came back to him; all that about

being humbled in order to be exalted, descending to mount and mounting to descend.

"I told you," he said, "that it's all part of the discipline. You can't escape it. You are cut off so that you may be brought nearer."

"But it doesn't bring me nearer. It's driving me away."

"It will. It will bring you. Wait."

"I have waited. I can't wait any longer. I can't go through with it a second time. I can *not* bear it. I cannot live like this."

"Come," he said, trying to be gentle and feeling furious. "You musn't say these things."

"If I only knew," she moaned, "what I'd done. There must be something. If I only knew what it is that comes between God and me."

"Try and think. Try and find out."

It was three minutes past four. If he didn't go now he would never go.

"You can't help me?"

"I can't help you more than I have done. It remains with you."

He felt that he must wean her from this habit of depending on him. And it was the surest way to make her go.

She faced him with a look so lost, so desperate that when he remembered it afterwards it stung him to compassion. But at the moment he missed it. He was thinking of Molly Beauchamp and how he could get to her before it was too late.

Inspiration came to him

"Pray," he said. "You have prayed that you may know God. Pray that you may know yourself. . . . And now I am really afraid I must be going."

And then a dreadful thought struck him. They would be going the same way. He didn't want to make for Queningford House accompanied by Agnes Lambert. He didn't want her to connect that urgency of his with Mrs. Beauchamp.

"But," he said, "if you will stay and rest here I will tell Pridget to bring you tea."

She protested. She wasn't tired. She didn't want any tea. He was firm.

"I insist. You must, really, to please me. I shall be less unhappy at leaving you. You *will?*"

He put a cushion at her back. "There," he said, "rest. Perhaps some thought will come to you."

She stayed and rested. After all, it was good to stay and rest there, in the place where his inner life, his true life, was lived; where he had prayed and meditated; where she could still feel the memory, almost the illusion, of his presence;

where she had come so many times for that communion with him that up till yesterday had always saved her.

Only now, she was past saving.

And this time Clement Chamberlain had given her no comfort. He had left her to herself. Like God, he had cast her off and forsaken her. She could hear his grave voice saying: "I can't help you more than I have done. It remains with you." And, "You have prayed that you may know God. Pray that you may know yourself."

He knew. *He* knew.

What was it that he knew? He must have seen something, some secret sin. *What?* What did he think of her that he should have said a thing like that?

That was the thought that came to her. Then suddenly she began to cry, like a hurt child, with helpless, choking sobs and hiccoughs. It would be awful if Pridget came in and found her crying. She got up and went away quietly, through the hall and out into the drive.

When she got to London Street she saw the Rector a long way in front of her, walking fast. She followed, keeping him in sight. She saw him stop at Queningford House. The door opened. He went in.

She stumbled up the stairs of her house and into her bedroom. She lay down on her bed, stretched out under the crucifix, and cried with a great, quiet crying of agony and despair. The darkness would never leave her. She was forsaken of God and forgotten. Alone among the dead.

The clock struck five. At that moment, in the house opposite, Clement Chamberlain held Molly Beachamp in his arm. They had agreed that they would be married at the end of May.

CHAPTER XIX

IT was nine o'clock in a perfect morning of June.

The Rector lay in the big double bed that had been brought from Queningford House. Downstairs nine deep, musical strokes of the hall clock told the hour. He woke suddenly with a queer mixed sense of familiarity and strangeness. It was his own old room, but it was another bed, a bed he had not slept in before, facing the door instead of the window. He yawned and stretched himself. His arm struck gently against a warm soft mass that he recognised as Molly, his wife. She lay there in the immense bed, with her back towards him, curled deliciously into a fat ball, her chin sunk to her breast, her knees drawn up to her waist and her heels to her hips: like a cat, he thought affectionately, or a dormouse; she ought to have had a furry tail to cuddle her little nose in. Between her blown cheeks her mouth was pushed out, half-open, breathing peacefully without a sound.

Peacefully; he had never known anybody so peaceful. Once fairly asleep this admirable woman lay beside him without a movement, breathing her noiseless breath. She gave him the double bliss of solitude and of companionship.

He raised himself on his elbow and stared at her. He could see the plaited roots of the thick rope of hair that disappeared under the bedclothes. He had got used to the sight of Molly in bed, but, every time, it gave him pleasure.

He looked at his watch. Nine o'clock. Breakfast was at nine. Gladys must have come in with the hot water an hour ago. The blinds were up and there was the brass can standing in the basin covered with a towel. They must have gone to sleep again after they were called.

It was his first married day at home after the three weeks' honeymoon. They had come back from the Riviera (Cap Martin) the night before. The sun shone. Through the open window the smell of roses and lavender came into the room and mixed with the smell of warm bed-clothes and of Molly's hair.

He stooped over her and kissed her and she woke, yawning like a little cat and rubbing her plump fists into her eyelids.

"Time to get up," he said.

"Oh, mutht we?"

"Nine o'clock."

"Ith it?" Her voice was sweet and thick, she lisped with drowsiness.

"Well, you can lie longer, dear, if you want to."

"No. We shall have to get up some time. May as well now. I want my breakfast."

"You can have it in bed."

"No, I'm lazy enough without that. I'd rather have it downstairs. With *you,* darling."

"You shall do as you like," he said and kissed her again. She was adorable. So soft, so plump, so sleepy.

He got up, dragging himself out of bed, and went into his dressing-room. His prie-Dieu and his cruicifix had been moved into it, and his old single bed where he had lain for a brief time last night.

He heard the soft thud of Molly's feet on the floor, as she rolled, unwillingly, out of bed. She would have her bath first, while he shaved and prayed. The religious rite followed close upon the other. He had got over the worst part of this unpleasant process of preparation for the day. He was not content to go through a mere form of words before his crucifix; he tried, con-

scientiously, to realise that he was in the presence of God every time; and it was very difficult.
He couldn't honestly say that he realised anything of the sort. Always he shrank from the
concentration and effort of shaving and of praying and always he enjoyed his hot bath and
brushing his hair.

The warmth and shining freshness of the
morning passed into his body. In the other room
he could hear Molly's feet pad-padding with an
unnatural quickness. The dear woman was
afraid that he would be down before her and that
she would keep him waiting for his breakfast.
He called out to her not to hurry, that he wasn't
dressed yet. He thought of Molly with tenderness. She didn't want him to feel that marriage
had brought the smallest discomfort or disorder
into his life.

And it hadn't. It was incredible how it had
intensified his peace and comfort. Molly was
peaceful and comfortable in herself and she
wanted everybody about her to be peaceful and
comfortable too.

He hurried a little in his dressing so as to be
down before her in time to pick a rose for her and
put it on her plate. He made a vow, then and
there, to bring her a flower every morning as

long as there were any flowers; in spring the first snowdrop, the first violet, in summer the first rose, in autumn the last rose and the first chrysanthemum. Except when it was cold and wet. She wouldn't expect it then.

He was putting the roses on her plate when he heard the soft thud of her feet on the stair. She was hurrying, hurrying to come to him.

"You needn't hurry, dear," he said. "In this house nobody hurries except the servants."

He put his arm in hers and led her out into the garden, and they went together to eat strawberries before breakfast. They picked them for each other. She chose the biggest and finest ones for him, and he chose the biggest and finest ones for her. Sometimes they disputed as to which *were* the biggest and finest, and when he said he had had enough she stood on tip-toe and pushed them into his mouth with her little fat fingers reddened with strawberry juice. He laughed, and they went in, laughing, to breakfast.

Breakfast was a splendid hope. He had acquired Radford by his marriage and he had yet to see whether her breakfasts equalled her luncheons and her dinners.

"Let us see," he said, "what Radford has given us."

She had given them a savoury omelette that caressed three senses, taste, touch and smell, and so hot that he could almost hear it hissing in the pan. And the coffee. He sniffed and a delicious, intoxicating thrill mounted into his brain. And as he looked across the table at Molly pouring it out, very serious, very careful to put in the right quantity of hot milk and cream, the right quantity of sugar, he thought of what Charlotte had said to him on his wedding-day. "You've done the best thing for yourself, Clement. But then you would." And she had asked him what he thought of the celibacy of the clergy *now?* And though Charlotte's congratulations had been double-edged, he owned that she was right.

Yes. He *had* done the best thing for himself, absolutely the best. It was Providential, the way things had turned out, as if all his life he had been saved for Molly. Supposing he had married poor Alice Vachell, would he have been happy and at peace, as he was at peace and happy now? However anxious she might have been to please him—and she would have been anxious—she would never have had Molly's sure and intimate knowledge of the things that pleased. Her anxiety, born of ignorance, would have destroyed all the pleasure. And Kitty Hancock—Kitty had been clearly inspired by Providence that day when she had taken him out to see her five children playing Cruggerhock. To think that he had actually been in danger of marrying Kitty.

And supposing he had married Agnes Lambert? Only he couldn't supose it. You couldn't marry Agnes Lambert.

As for the celibacy of the clergy, he could see now that he had been all wrong there. Good for some clergymen, for men like Jackman, but not for him. The efficiency of the clergy was what mattered, and marriage made for greater efficiency. He was twice the man he had been since he had married Molly. Fitter in every way. A better appetite, and clearer headed.

The blessed day went on. He sat all morning in his study reading a novel that his wife had recommended (he could trust her judgment), while Molly sat opposite him, knitting a jumper. She did this noiselessly, with only an occasional subdued click of her needles, reminding him that she was there. And from her large, ruminant eyes, and the cherub rose of her mouth, from all her quiet, gently voluptuous person there came, and hung about her, sweetness and comfort and peace like an essence, an emanation. She could sit like that for hours together, without speaking. When he looked up from his book she had a smile ready for him, a little struggling, infantile smile, crushed between her cheeks.

The morning passed in this silence and rest, this intimate communion of satisfied senses. They ate together an inimitable luncheon. For Radford's genius was dependent on the Rector's appreciation for the spurt that set it going. Molly said she would never have known what was *in* Radford, if she hadn't married him.

After luncheon they lay out under the beech tree, the Rector on one long chair and Molly on another. In all her attitudes there was an exquisite indolence. Pridget brought them their coffee there. And they began to talk. About the things they had done together in the Riviera; about the superiority of Radford's cooking to the cooking of the chef at the Cap Martin Hotel; about letting Queningford House furnished; about the places they could go and see now that "they" had "their" car. The Rector protested that the car was Molly's and Molly said that was all stuff and nonsense. What was his was hers and what was hers was his.

Her voice had begun to get thick and husky. It said "what'th" and "yourth" and "ith." It sounded further and further off; his own voice sounded further. Puffs of sleepy scent came from the roses and lavender in the beds above the lawn. The river kept up a sleepy gurgling as it flowed under the low wall at the bottom of the garden. The conversation died a delicious, drowsy death. They dozed.

Molly was the first to drop off. He had one clear moment in which he saw her surrendered. He yielded, voluptuously, to the overpowering suggestion and dropped off too.

He woke first. Molly was now fast asleep. She lay with her head tilted back on the cushions, her mouth half open, the full white slope of her throat trembling slightly with her breath. He looked at her. She was so innocent, so helpless, lying there in her sleep. He was overcome by his sense of Molly and of his love for her. She was his wife and he loved her. He could hardly believe it, yet so it was. Her sleep was so sound that she did not stir when Pridget brought out the tea-table.

The Rector sighed; for he found all emotion, even his own, oppressive. He got up, took a plate from the table and went into the kitchen garden. And there he stooped in the hot sun, he went stooping down the long rows of the strawberry bed, fumbling under the leaves, picking strawberries for Molly. He put the plate beside her on the table to greet her waking eyes.

Presently there was a soft, expanding movement in the mass that was Molly; she opened her eyes and sat up.

"Bless me," she said. "It isn't tea-time?"

"It is."

"Have I been asleep?"

"Yes."

"I hope I didn't do it with my mouth open?"

"Only a little open. You did it very prettily. Look what I've brought you."

"Strawberries? Oh, you darling."

Her throat made a little eager, swallowing movement. When they had finished the strawberries they waited for tea.

After tea they drove in the Rolls-Royce, along the wide, grass-bordered roads, between fields smelling of charlock and clover and mown hay.

Then the climax of dinner. Then the long, quiet evening, the innocent talk, the happy silences. Then ten o'clock striking and their eyes met.

"I think——"

"Shall we——?"

She rose and he followed as she went, slowly, with her rolling, padding motion, upstairs.

It had been a perfect day.

His second day was not quite so perfect. It began after breakfast, too soon after breakfast, with a visit from Mr. Thompson, the clergyman who had taken his duty during his honeymoon. Mr. Thompson was another Cartwright. He had worked hard, taking Miss Lambert's duty as well as the Rector's. It made him feel tired only to hear how hard Mr. Thompson had been working.

And Mr. Thompson was determined to tell him all about it; he didn't spare him a single visit he had paid.

Miss Lambert, he said, had not been able to do anything in the parish.

"Dear me," said the Rector, "how's that?"

"Well, I'm afraid she's in a very sad state."

"She must be ill indeed to give up her work."

"Quite unfit for anything."

"Do you know what's the matter with her?"

"I understand it's a complete nervous breakdown. Not altogether unexpected, Dr. Lawson tells me."

"You don't say so. This—this is very distressing."

"It began, I believe, with religious depression."

Mr. Thompson seemed to imply that it had not ended there.

"It began?" The Rector repeated. "Do you mean it's something worse than that?"

Mr. Thompson hesitated. "I don't know exactly what it is. Naturally I didn't like to ask. But I gather there has been some sort of mental disturbance."

"What is being done for her?"

"The Lawsons are taking care of her. She is with them now."

"Has Lawson consulted anybody?"

"Yes. I believe there was a consultation the other day. I think they are arranging to send her away somewhere. To some nursing home. The trouble is that the poor lady isn't very willing to go."

The Rector said it was very terrible and that he would try and see Lawson. He spoke as if this might be difficult, owing to the pressure of parish affairs. The fact was, the idea of seeing Lawson was excessively disagreeable to him. He spent the early half of the afternoon visiting his parish, which made it impossible for him to see Lawson then. And afterwards, what with the heat, and what with the unpleasantness of visiting, he wasn't fit for anything but sitting out with Molly in the garden.

Now the worst of the Rectory garden was that

anybody sitting out in it could be distinctly seen from the drive in front of the house. Therefore, the Rector was in the habit of sitting with his back turned to the drive, so that, although other people might see him, as he couldn't see them, he was not obliged to know that they were there.

This afternoon he sat with his back to the drive and Molly faced it. They waited for tea.

It was nearly tea-time when the sudden turn and stare of Molly's eyes towards the drive made him aware of danger.

"What is it?" he asked uneasily.

"A caller."

"I can't see anybody. I'm worn out."

"You shan't," she said; "I'll see her."

"Do you know who it is?"

"I think—I'm not sure, but I think—it's Miss Lambert."

He made as if he would have risen.

"Then—I'm afraid I must see her."

"Oh no, darling, you musn't. It'll worry you. I'll go to her."

And she went.

Miss Lambert waited in the drawing-room. Thin in her straight black gown that was like a nun's habit. A small silver crucifix hung on her flat breast. Her face was reddened and glazed,

her eyes shrunk and strained, small with weep-
ing; she trembled as she turned and saw the Rector's wife.

Up to this moment Molly had never paid any
attention to Miss Lambert, or her appearance;
now she was shocked into pity. It would be awful to have to tell her that she couldn't see Clement, but she felt that Miss Lambert in her present state was not a sight that Clement would have
wished to see.

Molly was very gentle, very kind. She held
the lean, shaking hand and pressed it in her
plump palm. Her voice was sweet and soothing.

"Dear Miss Lambert, how good of you to call."

She had decided that it would be more tactful
to take it as a call that was owing to the Rector's
wife.

"I'm afraid," Miss Lambert said, "it isn't a call
—exactly."

"No? Did you want to see the Rector?"

"I do. If he can—if he is not engaged."

"Well, he's not engaged; but he's resting. I'm
afraid I musn't let him see anybody. Is it anything I can do?"

"No. No. Nothing. Thank you. I wouldn't
have kept him long."

"I'm sorry. But just at this moment I want him

to rest. He was travelling all night before we came down. He's had a very hard day and he's tired out.

"No. No. I wouldn't think——" She drew herself up with a certain dignity. "I won't keep you."

"Oh, but you'll stay and have tea with me?"

"No, thank you, it's very kind, but I must be going."

And then, whether moved by a memory of the times when she used to have tea with Clement Chamberlain, or by sheer physical exhaustion, Miss Lambert began to cry.

"I'm sorry," she said. "I didn't mean to do that."

"I do it myself," said Molly, soothing her. "One can't help it sometimes when one's run down. You've been working too hard. I know what it is."

She didn't know that Miss Lambert had been "doing it," off and on, for two months, ever since the day in April when she had followed Clement Chamberlain and seen him go into Queningford House.

Miss Lambert went on crying and Molly weakened. Her softness could never hold out against other people's tears.

"If it's something *very* urgent I think Clement would like to see you."

But Miss Lambert's instinct for saving the Rector was stronger even than her desire to see him.

"I wouldn't for worlds have him disturbed," she said.

"Can I give him any message?"

"No. No, thank you. Perhaps, if he's rested tomorrow I might see him then."

"He shall call himself and see you early tomorrow afternoon."

She reflected that if Miss Lambert called on Clement he mightn't be able to get rid of her for ages, whereas if Clement called on Miss Lambert he could leave the minute he wanted to.

"Does he know," said Miss Lambert, "that I'm staying with the Lawsons?"

"He hasn't said anything about it."

"Then they haven't told him that I'm going away?"

"I don't think so."

"I'm not at all sure that I shall go. It depends on him."

"On Clement?"

"Yes."

"Then I'm sure he won't want you to go."

"If I were only sure——"

"You may be."

Miss Lambert rose and held out her hand.

"I can't let you go like this," Molly said. "Do let me bring you some tea."

"No, thank you. I couldn't drink it."

"Then stay and rest here till—till——" She didn't like to say "till you've left off crying."

But Miss Lambert wouldn't stay.

Molly went with her to the door and down the drive. As she opened the wide green gate to let her through into the market place she saw Mrs. Lawson standing on her own doorstep, looking up and down the street. When she caught sight of Miss Lambert she came to her, took her by the arm and led her back gently into the doctor's house.

Molly returned to her place on the lawn.

The Rector looked up at her uneasily. Her saddened face was the first intimation of unpleasantness.

"Well," he said, "so you've managed it?"

"Yes. I've managed it. It's just as well you didn't see the poor thing. She was crying."

"Crying?"

"Yes. She looks as if she'd been crying for months. She's cried her eyes away."

"Perhaps—I ought to have seen her."

"I said you'd go and see her tomorrow."

"Certainly I'll go and see her tomorrow."

"You know she's staying with the Lawson's?"

"Yes. They're taking care of her."

"Clement—what *is* the matter with her?"

"Oh—religious depression."

"It didn't look like religion to me," said Molly.

"I don't want to talk about her," he said, and Molly left off talking.

Tea time passed, and dinner time and the quiet evening. It was at ten minutes to ten, when they were both thinking of going to bed, that Dr. Lawson called.

He was in the study. He had said he wished to see Canon Chamberlain alone. The Rector, full of misgiving, went to him there. It was like Lawson to call at this unearthly hour. He just took any time that happened to be most convenient to himself. No sort of consideration for other people.

"Well, Lawson, what is it?" he said, with his genial air of willingness to help.

"I want you to give me a letter for Agnes Lambert."

"For Agnes Lambert?"

"Yes. We're going to get her away tomorrow

to a nursing home in Cheltenham. We've arranged to start first thing in the morning."

"Yes?"

"It was all settled. And now she says she won't go unless it's your wish. I want you to write to her and say it is your wish."

"But that—that is a very unpleasant thing for me to do."

"I don't care how unpleasant it is. It's got to be done. It's the only thing that'll get her off."

"Tomorrow morning? But I promised to call and see her in the afternoon."

"Really, Canon Chamberlain, it'll be much better for her not to see you. I think we've made her see that. She hasn't been herself, you know, since she first heard you were going to be married."

"My dear Lawson, you don't mean to say *that's* affected her?"

"I mean to say that's what's the matter with her."

"Does she know it?"

"I can't say. I don't think so. They don't always know. In her case it's camouflaged as religious depression. That saves her face, poor thing."

"You said you'd made her see it."

"That you're bad for her? I meant your religious influence."

"I had no other."

"That was quite enough."

"I assure you, Lawson, I never did anything or said anything to—to make her think——"

"No, you didn't do *that*."

"What *did* I do?"

"Well, if you want to know, you did everything you could to encourage her in her delusion."

"Not that delusion."

"I'm referring to her religious ideas. You worked on her feelings——"

"I? *I* worked on her feelings? I never——"

"Pardon me, Canon Chamberlain, you did. You kept her in a perpetual state of excitement and exaltation. You encouraged her in her morbid mysticism. I've seen the books you lent her."

"I lent her the classic books on a subject she was interested in."

"I don't say they'd have done a sound person any harm. But in her state they were enough to turn her brain. You might as well have given her poison. Better. That would have ended it."

"Really, Lawson, this is a most unfair attack. I decline to accept any responsibility."

"I'm afraid you must accept some. You were warned of the consequences if you encouraged her. You went on encouraging her. I begged you not to keep her here if I could persuade her to go away. We might have got her out of the place before your marriage if it hadn't been for you. But what did you do? You actually persuaded her to stay."

"I did it for the best, Lawson."

"When you'd been told it was for the worst. No. I'm sorry, Canon, but I'm afraid I can't let you off. Still, the harm's done now and we must try and undo it as far as possible."

"Have you any hope of her recovery?"

"Yes. With proper care."

"And what do you want me to do? I'm in your hands, doctor."

"I want you to write her a letter saying that you wish her to go away."

"I'll write it at once."

He was anxious now to dissociate himself entirely from Miss Lambert's ideas, to undo any possible harm that he might have done. Not that he admitted that he had done any harm, except that he could see of course it would have been better if he had persuaded her to leave two months ago. But we cannot be wise all the time.

He wrote:

"My dear Miss Lambert:

I hear that you want to know whether it is my wish that you should go away. For your own sake only, it is my wish. Sorry as we shall be to lose you, I feel that you would do well to leave a place that must have so many associations with your illness, and that change of air and new surroundings are essential to your recovery. I hope you will submit in every way to those who are taking care of you, who are only thinking of your good.

Before you go I must thank you once more for all that you have done in Queningford. You will be greatly missed.

My thoughts are with you.

Most sincerely yours,
Clement Purcell Chamberlain."

"For Goodness' sake," said Dr. Lawson. "Don't say anything about God."

"I haven't mentioned him."

He handed him the letter, open, for him to read.

"Will that do?"

"Er—admirably."

"I admit that I ought to have written it two months ago, but one cannot be wise for everybody all the time."

"By the way," he said. "How is she going?"

"That's the worst of it. My car's broken down or I'd have driven her myself. I shall have to take the King's Head car. I wish we could have done without the King's Head people."

"I'm sure my wife would lend her car."

"That would be very good of her."

"It shall be round at what hour?"

"Eight sharp. I must be back in time for my patients."

"You may depend on Rendall."

At the front door he added, "I'm very much upset about all this."

"So am I," said the doctor as he went.

Clement Chamberlain returned to the drawing-room.

"My dear," said Molly, "what is it?"

Then he told her. He told her everything. He cast from him the long tradition of clerical reticence. He wanted her comfort.

"And Lawson holds me responsible," he said.

"I never heard such ridiculous nonsense. I'm

very sorry for the poor lady, but how on earth you could help her falling in love with you—or how she could help it, for that matter—— Responsibility indeed! Let's go to bed."

And they went.

Early in the morning they were wakened by the "honk-honk" of the car as it drove from the Rectory gate to the doctor's house to call for Miss Lambert. After a short silence they heard it sounding again at the corner of the Green Dragon and again at the bridge as it rushed up Drayton Street towards Cheltenham, taking her away.

It was later on that they heard, through Kitty Hancock, who had it from Mrs. Lawson who had it the doctor, that the drive to Cheltenham had been awful. Agnes Lambert had cried all the time and had kept on saying, "He's sending me away. He's sending me away. What have I done that he should send me away?" The poor thing thought that it was a plot hatched among them to get rid of her, to please the Rector and Mrs. Chamberlain.

"It was a great mistake," Kitty said, "to have taken her in the Rectory car."

When Kity had gone, the Rector and his wife looked at each other.

"*Was* it a mistake?" she said.

"Perhaps. Who knows what was in her poor head. Molly, I wouldn't for the world this should have happened. She—she was the gentlest thing I've ever known."

"She *was* gentle."

"Well, it's all over."

Then a thought came to him. His actual loss.

"I don't know what I shall do without her in the parish."

"You'll have to get a second curate, dear. We can afford it now. It's what you ought to have had all along. After all," she said, "Miss Lambert couldn't take the Services."

"Don't, Molly. I don't want to speak of her again."

It was too unpleasant.

CHAPTER XX

THE parish had hardly got used to the Rector's marriage and Miss Lambert's removal when there was more excitement. It came at the June Quarter when Queningford House was let to Mrs. Rivers. She had taken it for the summer and autumn. She was tired of wandering, she said; her husband was coming home from Mesopotamia and she must have a decent place for him to come to. Peter was fond of Queningford. She was expecting him every day.

Kitty Hancock had spread the legend of Sylvia's passionate devotion to her husband, and you would have thought that if anything could have made her happy, it was the prospect of seeing him again. But with each day Mrs. Rivers looked sadder and more mysterious than ever.

"I can't imagine what's the matter with Sylvia," her cousin Molly said. "You'd think Peter was just going out to Mespot instead of coming back."

The Rector and his wife had agreed that there was something they disliked about Sylvia, something that made them feel uncomfortable.

"I can get on with most people," Molly said, "but Sylvia and I never hit it off together."

"I don't care for her. She's the sort of woman I wouldn't like to be left alone in the room with."

"You shan't be left alone with her. But I don't think many men would feel like that. You can't say Sylvia isn't fascinating."

"She's repellent to me," said the Rector.

"Well, anyhow, Peter adores her. And she adores Peter. I never saw two people more devoted to each other."

"I don't doubt it for a moment. It's simply that I don't care for these mysterious women. You can never tell what they're thinking. It's like a cat in the room."

"Oh, well, I dare say she'll be different when Peter comes back. It's been pretty awful for her these two years. I don't know how *I* should feel if *my* husband was out in Mespot for two years."

"I ought to be thinking of my sermon," he said.

"Well, I'll leave you in peace. I've just got time before dinner to run over to Kempston and see Kitty."

A CURE OF SOULS

It was six o'clock on a Saturday afternoon. He had been lying out in the garden all day, and he had not even thought of his sermons until now. The Rector had a certain pride in his preaching and in the series that he thought of as Queningford Sermons. Still, he could always fall back on an old one. So he lay out in the garden a little longer and it was past seven before he withdrew into his study. And dinner was at a quarter to eight.

No. He wouldn't write any fresh sermons; he would simply go over the old ones and consider which he would preach tomorrow. There was one on a text in the Epistle for Evensong. I. John, iv. 8. "He that loveth not, knoweth not God; For God is love." Most suitable for Evensong.

He was still trying to find another equally suitable for Matins when he heard the front door bell ringing. He felt safe, for it could hardly be a caller at that late hour.

And yet—and yet—he could hear feet in the hall that were not Pridget's feet; the drawing-room door opened and shut and Pridget came to him.

"Mrs. Rivers to see you in the drawing-room, sir."

"Mrs. Rivers?"

She must have come with some message for Molly.

"Yes, sir."

"What time is it?"

"Twenty past seven, sir."

"Very well. Tell Mrs. Rivers I will be with her in one minute."

He had his hand on the wrong sermon, the one he had preached last Sunday on Confession. "If we confess our sins he is faithful and just to forgive us our sins and to cleanse us from all unrighteousness."

Ah—this would do: the Sermon on Responsibility. "Am I my brother's keeper?" He would just glance over it and the thing would be done with.

He glanced over it and the clock struck half past seven. He was then aware that he was spinning out the time, putting off the moment when he would have to see Mrs. Rivers, hoping that at any minute Molly would come in, so that he wouldn't have to see her alone. But if he didn't see her at once it would be dinner time before he could get rid of her. He went.

Mrs. Rivers sat in an ominous, brooding attitude, and so that he saw her sideways as he came in. She started at the opening of the door and her face showed an agitation that frightened and embarrassed him. She seemed, in her profound pre-occupation, to have no idea of the lateness of the hour.

He apologised for keeping her waiting on the grounds that he was busy with his sermon.

"Did you come to see Molly? She's out, but she'll be back any minute."

"No. I didn't come to see Molly. I came to see you. Can I see you alone?"

"Certainly. We *are* alone."

"But somebody may come in—Molly——"

Yes. Molly might come in any minute.

"We can go into the study," he said. "And I'll leave word that I'm engaged."

He was trapped. Not even Molly's return would bring him deliverance.

He took her into the study. She had made no attempt as yet to account for her appearance. It was evident that she was in a state beyond all trivial explanations and apologies.

"I wanted to see you alone," she said, "because I've something to tell you. Something I want your advice about."

He replied, as he had replied in so many cases, that she should have the best advice he could give her; if he could advise at all. In spite of his dislike and of his fear, she had roused his curiosity. He was not unwilling to hear what she had to say, if only she would be quick and get it over. And he wished that she could have chosen another time.

"I ought to tell you at once that I have a confession to make."

He bowed his head.

"A rather terrible confession." As she spoke a sudden calmness came to her.

"Indeed? Are you quite sure you ought to make it?"

"No. But I'm quite sure I *must* make it."

"Well—— And are you equally sure that I am the right person to make it to?"

"Is one sure of anything? Of anybody?"

"I mean, what made you think of coming to me? Was it the Sermon I preached last Sunday? Because I spoke only of confession to God."

"I'm afraid I wasn't thinking of the sermon. I was thinking of something Kitty said about you once. That if ever she had anything awful to confess, she'd want to confess it to you."

"Kitty is sometimes apt to say things she doesn't mean."

"She meant it that time. She said it was because you wouldn't be carried away by any feeling, and because you'd probably forget all about it the next minute. I want somebody like that, who won't have any feeling, who'll forget —who won't care enough to remember."

"And you think I should meet the case?"

"I think you would be absolutely impersonal."

"I'll try to be if that will help you."

"And you won't preach to me? You'll give me the advice of a man of the world? Not clergyman's advice."

"I can't promise that it won't be 'clergyman's advice.' It will be sensible advice, I hope, if that's what you mean."

"It is what I mean. I needn't ask you not to tell a soul. Not even Molly. I know you're safe."

"You certainly needn't. Whatever you say, it shall be sacred."

"If only," she said, "I knew how to begin. You see, it's not as if you knew anything about me."

"One moment. Have you really thought it well over? I don't want you to yield, in a state of emotion, to an impulse you may afterwards regret."

"I've thought till I'm ill with thinking."

She paused.

The honking of the car was heard and its rush to the door. It was followed by the clang of the dressing bell, ten minutes late. Mrs. Rivers took no notice of these things. She sat still, in a dreadful stormy stillness.

And a disturbing thought came to the Rector. It was now twenty to eight; dinner would be ready in five minutes; but in five minutes Mrs. Rivers couldn't possibly be gone. She hadn't even begun her confession. And the confession, when it came, whatever it was, would have to be weighed and looked at all round, advice would have to be given, argued about (women always argued about advice); the arguments would have to be met and overcome; anything might follow. He was in for another forty minutes of it, half an hour at the very least. The dinner would be done to a turn at this moment; and in half an hour it would be spoiled.

For Radford had three terrible faults; pride, self-importance and bad temper. Pride in her cooking so great that she considered that a dinner was slighted if you were five minutes late for it; self-importance so supreme that she resented a slight to her dinner as an insult to herself; temper so bad that she revenged herself on you by letting the dinner spoil rather than keep it back; so that you were punished where you had sinned.

And tonight he was going to be at least five and twenty minutes late.

Mrs. Rivers began again suddenly.

"Canon Chamberlain—you know my husband is coming here?"

"I had heard so. We are rejoiced. When do you expect him?"

That instant he thought he saw a way of getting out. If Mrs. Rivers wanted advice, Colonel Rivers was the proper person for her to go to.

"Any day, almost any minute."

"Then, my dear Mrs. Rivers, would it not be better for you to consult him? Surely your husband is the proper person to give you advice."

Mrs. Rivers laughed, a queer, harsh laugh, unpleasant and mysterious. He was reminded again of her mystery.

"You don't know what you're talking about?" she said. "That's the whole point—whether I must tell him or not."

He sniffed inaudibly. That roast chicken was

done to a turn. It wanted now but two minutes to the quarter. His mind wandered.

"Canon Chamberlain," she said again, turning his attention from the delicious aroma that had captured it—"I've been unfaithful to my husband."

He gave a start, deliberately contrived to show the shock of his amazement.

"Dear me, dear me, this is very terrible." He was going to say, "Are you quite sure you've been unfaithful?" when he remembered that people like Mrs. Rivers didn't make that sort of statement unless they were sure. "Very terrible indeed."

"I know it's awful. I'm not going to excuse myself. It just happened. I couldn't stand living without Peter. And Charlie was there. Charlie Hancock, Kitty's brother-in-law."

"But how——"

"I don't know how it happened. It just seemed the only thing that could happen.

"The only thing? It didn't occur to either of you to exercise self control."

"All sorts of things occurred to us. Only they didn't seem to matter. Nothing seemed to matter while Peter was away. And now he's coming back—and—I'm frightened."

"I'm afraid you deserve to be frightened."

He didn't feel inclined to spare her. He was annoyed with Mrs. Rivers for committing adultery, still more annoyed with her for confessing her adultery to him and for spoiling his dinner. Sitting there before him, in her terrible calmness, she seemed to him shameless. Her sadness and her mystery were gone. She was common, shameless and common. Her very beauty irritated him, it was so tranquil, so assured, so untouched by any sense of sin.

"You needn't tell me what I deserve," she said. "I know all about that. The question is, what am I to do about it?"

"Do about it? The first thing you have to do is to give up that man."

"Charlie? I have given him up. And then?"

"Go back to your husband—if he'll have you."

"And if he won't have me? Go back to Charlie?"

"Go back to a decent life, Mrs. Rivers, and forget him."

"It isn't so easy as all that. Even if I could forget him."

"You *must* forget him. You must pray to God to make you forget him. Before you came to confess to me did you confess your sin to God? This is a very awful sin against God, you know."

"It's the awful sin against Peter that bothers me. It would be so simple if—if I didn't love Peter."

"It's a strange way of loving your husband, to go off with another man."

"It does seem strange, doesn't it? But that's how it is. If I could have borne to live without Peter I wouldn't have gone to Charlie. How *can* I make you understand it when you don't feel?"

"You are greatly mistaken, Mrs. Rivers. I can and do feel."

"Not that way."

"Well—not that way, I hope."

"You see," she went on, "I only wanted Charlie when Peter wasn't there. At least I thought I wanted him. I suppose I did in a way. I might still if it wasn't for Peter. The very minute I heard Peter was coming home I *knew* I cared for him more than anything in the world. I want so awfully to go back to him."

And as if she hadn't done enough already to upset him, Mrs. Rivers began to cry. She did it without sobbing or struggling, with lips thinned and tight shut, resisting deformity, with no movement but a slight shuddering of her body and the brimming, falling and brimming of her tears. She dried them with a slow, efficient pressure of her pockethandkerchief; the gesture seemed to say that crying called for no comment, it was as simple and inevitable as sinning. It just happened. All the same, he turned away from it as he would have turned from some indecency.

Suddenly she started.

"Isn't that Molly coming?"

She was uneasy now, her nerves on edge; she had heard Molly's soft padding.

He got up and looked out into the hall as Molly closed the drawing-room door behind her.

"No," he said, "she has gone into the drawing-room."

She was there, waiting for him, waiting for her dinner. The hall was full of the smell of chicken roasting too long; in fancy he could see the sweet flesh dried, the golden skin darkening, crackling, unbasted. There was a smell, no less poignant, of roast potatoes hardening in the pan.

Mrs. Rivers looked up.

"Please listen to me," she said.

"I *am* listening." It seemed to him that his patience with this woman was more than human.

"I don't want sympathy," she said. "I don't care what you think of me."

"I am not reproaching you."

"I don't care if you do reproach me. I don't care what anybody thinks. I'm past caring."

"If I could only feel that you were sorry."

"Sorry? What does my being sorry matter? Nothing matters but Peter. I only want to know one thing. If I go back to him shall I have to tell him?"

"Certainly you will have to tell him."

"I can't," she said. "Nobody knows. If I don't tell him he'll never know. Why should I make him miserable?"

Now the Rector in his long experience had found that if you give people the advice they want they'll come to you again the next time for more of the same kind; while, if you give them the advice they don't want, the chances are you have got rid of them forever. He was determined that Mrs. Rivers should not come to him again. On the other hand, if he satisfied her she would be more likely to go at once. But his conscience would not allow him to counsel a deception. He must struggle against this laziness that urged him to the easier way. He must go through with it.

"You have asked my advice," he said. "I can't help it if it's not the advice you wanted."

"But how can I tell Peter I've been unfaithful to him? How *can* I?"

"How can you live with a lie between you? How can you bear to deceive a man who trusts you? That lie will eat into your lives and poison them. You will never be able to forget what you have done. You will feel far more dishonoured by deceit than by confession. But if you are brave and tell him the truth, like an honourable woman, and he forgives you and takes you back, then, and then only you may feel as if it had never been."

"No. Then I shall feel as if it were going on all the time. He'll be thinking of it. I'll be thinking of it. Perhaps he'll be afraid I shall do it again. Perhaps I'll be frightened into doing it. But if I knew he didn't know, I should be safe, I should be happy."

"No. You would not be safe, *or* happy. You only think you would be."

The clock struck eight. He knew now that he had taken a disastrous line, a line that prolonged the interview. But he had to stick to it.

"Believe me, it is the wrong unconfessed that stays in our minds forever. And what right have you to deceive him? To come to him as an innocent woman when you are not innocent? Unfaithfulness is bad enough without adding to it that lie. How will you be able to face your husband when you think of what you've done? When you think of the lie you are living night and day? I should have thought that any pain would be more bearable than that."

"You don't know Peter."

"No. But, if Colonel Rivers is the man I think he is, he will be glad that you have saved yourself that pain. Whereas if he thought that you had deceived him——"

"He wouldn't think it."

"You don't know. Your sin may be found out. Mr. Hancock has been staying with you."

"With a crowd of other people."

"Who may have seen something. They may have seen more than you think."

Mrs. Rivers rose.

"Kitty was right," she said. "You have no pity."

"Indeed I have pity. But I cannot advise you

against my conscience. Cannot you see that your silence is dishonouring to your husband and yourself?"

"Yes, I do see it. But—I can't tell him."

"Ah—you will only take the advice that is pleasant to yourself."

"No. No. I want to do the straight thing if I can."

"Then do it. Promise me you will do it."

"I promise you I won't deceive Peter."

"That's right. It's the only honourable thing."

At last. At last it was over. She was going.

He took the hand she held out to him. He went with her to the house door.

As he returned there came towards him from the open kitchen the smell of roast chicken singed: ruined beyond redemption.

CHAPTER XXI

BY Monday evening everybody had heard that Mrs. Rivers had travelled up to London with Mr. Hancock on Sunday, by the Swindon train, driving to the Junction shamelessly and openly in the King's Head car. A week later everybody knew that they had gone abroad together. And everybody said it was a sad home-coming for Colonel Rivers. He had arrived early in the week following the flight to London. Kitty had had to meet him at Southampton with the news. The few people who were lucky enough to have caught sight of him described him as completely broken down.

But the Colonel didn't give them much time to observe him, for he left Queningford after three days of it, unable to endure a place he associated with his wife's unfaithfulness. The question was, would he divorce her? Curiosity remained unsatisfied on this point. If Mrs. Hancock and the Chamberlains knew anything they kept it to themselves. As Mrs. Rivers was

Mrs. Chamberlain's first cousin it was felt that she had brought scandal into the Rectory itself.

These exciting events diminished the interest that would otherwise have been taken in Kitty Hancock's engagement to Mr. Cartwright, following his appointment to the living of Colne Cerney, a village not far from Queningford.

He arrived at his Vicarage in time to take part in the Dedication Service for the Unveiling of the Queningford-cum-Kempston Maisey War Memorial.

Town and countryside were moved to such enthusiasm that the scandal of Mrs. Rivers was forgotten, the old dispute with the Rector was forgotten, and all differences of feeling were laid aside. The church was packed with county people, townspeople, people from every village in the parish, carrying bunches of flowers, wreaths of flowers, wreaths of laurel. The Nonconformists had accepted the Rector's cordial invitation to attend the Dedication Service, and he was much gratified to see that they were there to a man, Wesleyans, Baptists and Congregationalists. The chancel was decorated with flags, scarlet and white; scarlet and white and blue; black, red and yellow, on the grey stone of the walls and the dark oak of the screen. The flags of the Allies, on forward slanting standards, hung on the south wall above the Memorial that was veiled with the Union Jack.

The great west door stood open, and at three o'clock there came a sound of singing from the churchyard outside.

> Onward, Christian so-o-o-oldiers
> Marching as to-o-War,
> With the cross of Je-sus
> Going on—before.

The procession entered, led by the tall cross that bowed forward, swaying slightly in the hands of the chorister. The choir followed, and after the choir the clergy of ten parishes, two abreast; after them Mr. Cartwright and Mr. Fawcett; and after Mr. Cartwright and Mr. Fawcett, the Rector alone; a stream of white surplices. And clergy and choir and congregation sang together.

> Fo'rward—in'to—ba-a-te'-el
> See His banners go.

> Crowns and thrones may pe-erish
> Kingdoms rise and wane,
> But the Church of Je-sus
> Constant will remain.

The Rector marched with bowed head, singing as he went. Wave after wave of emotion rolled through him, flushing his face. This moment and the next and the next were his, up to the supreme climax of his sermon. He had dreaded and desired this day; dreaded it because he shrank from all emotional disturbance, desired it because he had made the Dedication Service a beautiful and impressive thing and his part in it would be beautiful and impressive.

The choristers parted, curving right and left into the choir stalls. The Rector and his curate and the clergy of ten parishes took their places.

Mr. Cartwright read the General Confession and the Absolution. Special Psalms were sung. The Rector had chosen them. "I will lift up mine eyes unto the hills:" "He that dwelleth in the secret place of the Most High:" "Blessed be the Lord my God who teacheth my hands to war and my fingers to fight." He was lifted again on wave after wave of emotion, carried away by the sound of his own deep chanting, and the deep and shrill chanting of the choir.

. . . "The Lord himself *is* thy keeper: the Lord is thy defence upon thy ri-ight hand

"So that the sun shall not burn thee by day: nei-ther the moon by night.

"The Lord shall preserve thee from all evil: yea, it is even he that shall keep thy soul. . . ."

"That our sons may grow up as the you-ung plants: and that our daughters may be as the polished corners *of* the temple.

"That our garners may be full and plenteous with all manner of store . . .

". . . that there be no decay, no leading into captivity, and no complaining *in* our streets."

And now the voice of Mr. Fawcett was heard reading the Lesson.

"And an high way shall be there, and a way, and it shall be called The way of holiness . . . the wayfaring men, though fools, shall not err therein . . . the redeemed shall walk there: and the ransomed of the Lord shall return and come with singing unto Zion; and everlasting joy shall be upon their heads: they shall obtain gladness and joy, and sorrow and sighing shall flee away."

As the Service composed itself before him, the Rector had a thrill of pride and satisfaction. There could hardly have been a more beautiful and impressive Service.

The Benedictus followed, then the Lord's Prayer and the Collect for Peace.

There was a solemn pause, a silence; and then a stir as the congregation turned where it knelt

towards the War Memorial hidden by its Union
Jack. General Sir Charles Philpot slipped from
his place and took his stand by the Memorial.
He released the cord; the veil fell; the decorated
stone canopy was revealed, and under it the roll
of the dead, on the white tablet, glittered through
the thick light.

And the Rector sent up his Prayer of Dedication.

"Lord of all power and might, we humbly
dedicate this Memorial to thy glory and to the
memory of all those of this parish who gave up
their lives for God and for their country in the
great war. We pray that their names may be
held in remembrance forever upon earth as their
souls are in thy heavenly Kingdom. Amen."

He stood up and read the long roll of the dead.
A hymn was sung.

> How bright those glorious spirits shine,
> Whence all their white array?
> How came they to the blissful seats
> Of everlasting day?

The Rector rose and made his way solemnly
to the pulpit; while the hymn lashed all his
nerves to disagreeable emotion.

It ceased. He stood up, waiting for his moment. He looked round at his congregation, summoning attention. He thrust out his breast. Pride swelled it as he saw his church so full. People standing in the side aisles. It was very gratifying. He paused till the stir that had followed his rising had died down. Then he gave out his text: "A great multitude that no man could number. . . . These are they which came out of great tribulation, and have washed their robes and made them white in the blood of the Lamb."

He touched, first of all, very tenderly, on the sorrow of those who had come there that day to celebrate the unveiling of this Memorial to their beloved dead. He spoke of the men, the husbands, the fathers, the brothers, the sons and the lovers, whose names were inscribed there for ever as a remembrance. He dwelt at some length on their sacrifice, and exhorted his congregation to live so that it might not have been made in vain. "Let us see to it that our lives which they saved by that sacrifice are worthy of it." He spoke of victory and the responsibilities of victory. And thus by a well regulated transition he returned to the War Memorial, and fairly let himself go in his peroration.

"And because patriotism is a holy thing, a

sacred thing, a religious thing, it was thought that no place was more fitting for this War Memorial than the place that we have given it to-day. We are thus paying our dead the very highest honour that was possible. Higher than if we had set up our Memorial in the market place. For the Church is above the market place, above the township, above the country, above the world. It takes to itself all the civic virtues; for duty to the Church of Christ includes all other duties. It takes to itself under its shelter and protection, the names of the glorious dead, as it takes their souls and keeps them in an everlasting remembrance. I would have you think of them, of that multitude which no man can number, not as inhabitants of this or that town, of this or that village, but as citizens of that Heavenly City which hath no foundations, whose builder and maker is God."

After the sermon came the Collection (when another hymn was sung) and after the offertory the Benediction.

Then from somewhere in the chancel a bugle sounded the Last Post and the Reveillée. It was all over.

Then came the procession of the congregation past the Memorial.

A CURE OF SOULS

It stood up, strange and new in the old church, with its clean cut triple canopy, the fretted arches and the pinacles edged with leaf work, beaded, curled, uncurling. A square tudor rose in scarlet and gold decorated the centre of each arch. Two clustered pillars sustained the canopy, their capitals supported, like the bows of a ship, on angels' heads, scarlet and gold. The stone tablet showed three lists of names in scarlet and gold lettering. A long stone shelf was placed underneath it for the offerings of flowers and wreaths. Two scarlet and gold lions, couching, appeared in high relief on the carved work of its base.

Shelf and base, and the floor in front of the Memorial were presently covered with flowers and wreaths. One by one the congregation, having laid down its offerings, passed out. The Fawcetts and Mr. Cartwright, Kitty Hancock and Hilda Wrinch, the Rector and Mrs. Chamberlain remained. Apart in the doorway, Sir Charles and Lady Philpot were congratulating the sculptor.

The Rector spoke first to Kitty Hancock. Her husband's name glittered from its place in the roll.

"Do you like it, Kitty?"

"Yes. And I love the names."

"It's pure Gothic of the Fifteenth Century."

He turned to Hilda.

"What do *you* think of it?"

"Oh, it's all right. Ripping architecture. But——"

"But what?"

"The church is so old and it's so new. It screams a bit, doesn't it?"

"Time will soften it."

"I hope time will soften the hearts of the Noncomformists."

"They were all here, Hilda."

"Yes. They were all here."

"You might leave that alone, I think, today."

And they all went over to the Rectory for tea. The ten clergymen from the neighbouring parishes joined them there. And everybody congratulated the Rector on his Dedication Service, his sermon and his Memorial. They spoke as if it were his.

An hour later, as they were all going, Kitty came to him.

"I want a talk with you sometime. When can I see you? Tomorrow?"

"Why not now?"

"No. Not now. Six o'clock tomorrow."

It was settled.

His instinct told him that the interview would not be agreeable. If the things that Kitty had to say to him could not be said at this hour, the hour of his solemn, sacred triumph, that was because they were unpleasant. She didn't like to dash him down when he was proud and happy.

Kitty was going to talk about Mrs. Rivers's affair; she was going to be unpleasant. Tomorrow at six o'clock.

He dreaded tomorrow.

Tomorrow came, and Kitty at six o'clock. He was shut up alone with her in his study for three quarters of an hour. And she was unpleasant. She started, without any gentle preliminaries, on Mrs. Rivers's affair.

"I needn't pretend that you don't know about it. Everybody does. Sylvia has been perfectly open and straightforward."

He raised his eyebrows. And she went on.

"She wrote to me that Sunday night and told me."

"You'd no idea what was going to happen?" he said.

"No. I hadn't. Because it needn't have happened. It wouldn't have happened if Sylvia had come to me instead of you."

"Did she tell you she came to me?"

"Yes. She told me what you said. It was all in that letter."

He was silent. He wondered. Surely, surely Kitty was not going to make *him* responsible for what had happened?

"Clement," she said, "what on earth possessed you to advise Sylvia to tell Peter?"

"My dear Kitty, what other advice could I have given her?"

"Good heavens, you could have given her the advice *I*'d have given her, to go back to Peter, since she loved him; and *since she loved him,* to say nothing."

"I couldn't advise her to deceive her husband, to go to him with that lie between them."

"Nonsense. She hadn't got to lie. Only to hold her tongue. She had a right to keep her secret."

"To deceive him?"

"If you put it that way. To keep him from knowing what was better for him not to know."

"I cannot agree with you. To me truth comes before everything."

"Before other people's happiness?"

"If their happiness means lying, yes. Truth's truth, Kitty."

"And what is truth?"

"You may well ask me."

"It seems to me that it takes two people to make truth. One to speak it and one to understand it. If I tell you a thing that's true in a way that makes you not understand it, I'm not telling the truth. I haven't allowed for your understanding."

"Well?" He wondered where she was coming out.

"Well—if Sylvia had told Peter what *you'd* call the truth, that she'd left him for Charlie Hancock, he wouldn't have understood it. He'd have gone off with the idea that Sylvia didn't care for him. Now, the truth is that Sylvia does care for Peter, more than for all the Charlie Hancocks in the world. At least that's the only truth that matters. So you see, truth would have been better served by saying nothing about it."

"Casuistry, my dear."

"It isn't. It's common sense. Couldn't you see that that's what Sylvia wanted—to say nothing? She only went to you to back her up because she wasn't in a state to decide anything for herself, poor darling."

"Your sister led me to believe that she was going back to her husband; and she promised me, she *promised* me she would not deceive him."

"She didn't go back to him, but she didn't deceive him. She took the middle course. She bolted, and told me to tell him she'd bolted. She couldn't face him with it."

"Why not?"

"Because he was afraid he wouldn't forgive her. She was afraid for her life of him. Peter's a perfect dear, but he's got the devil of a temper."

"Oh. Still, Kitty, she should have risked it."

"Sylvia isn't a brave woman, and the risk was awful. *Now* you see what you had hold of, and look at the mess you've made of it. The ghastly mess. Sylvia wretched. Peter wretched; when they might have been happy. Nobody happy but that beast Charlie, who doesn't deserve to be. And *he* won't be happy very long. Really, I can't forgive you."

"You are very hard on me, Kitty."

"No, Clement. It's you who are hard. Hard as nails. If you'd cared a rap about Sylvia you'd have paid more attention to the circumstances; you'd have *seen*. But you're too lazy to care."

"I couldn't have done more than I did."

"Oh yes, you could. And it's always the same.

It was the same with the War Memorial. You were too lazy to care about other people's feelings, so you did what nobody wanted done. Yes, I know it's a beautiful War Memorial, and everything went off splendidly yesterday, but it isn't the thing they wanted."

"You needn't cast that up to me again."

"I'm casting it up because it's of a piece with all the rest. It was the same with Billy Cartwright. Everybody wanted him to stay and he didn't want to go, but you made him, because you couldn't bear his trying to wake you up. It was the same with Agnes Lambert. She wouldn't be in a nursing home now if you'd taken care of her."

Kitty had turned against him, too.

"Really Kitty, I decline to be responsible for Agnes Lambert, or for your sister either."

"Still, you *are* responsible. You're a parson. Billy says that parsons can only justify their existence nowadays by taking care of people who can't take care of themselves. Agnes Lambert couldn't. Sylvia couldn't. And they came to you to help them, trusting you. What have you done to them?"

"You're bitter, Kitty. How is it? You used not to be."

"I'm not bitter. How could I be bitter when I'm going to marry Billy? I'm only telling you the *truth*. Nobody else will."

She rose and looked at him.

"A cure of souls, Clement, is a cure of souls. You can't get out of it."

"Have I ever tried to get out of it?"

"Have you ever been in it, really *in* it?"

When she had gone he sat in his study, thinking. His thoughts were even more unpleasant than Kitty's words. The high waves of emotion that had uplifted him yesterday were spent. The ebb sucked him under, carried him he knew not where.

Kitty had said he wasn't fit to have a cure of souls. Charlotte had said it. He wondered: Was it true? Had he never really been "in it"?

And because he couldn't bear to be left alone with his wonder, he went into the drawing-room to Molly. The evening had turned chilly and she sat there before a fire.

"Well?" she said. "What had Kitty got to say? Something unpleasant?"

"Very unpleasant."

"About Sylvia?"

"And about everything. Kitty has been pitching into me all round. She told me I was re-

sponsible for Sylvia's running away with Charlie
Hancock, and for Agnes Lambert's break-down.
I'm responsible for everything that's gone wrong
in this parish since I came into it."

"Well, it was very impertinent of Kitty, and
you're no more responsible than I am. But as
long as you remain in the Church, Clement, you'll
be *held* responsible. People *will* say these things.
They can't forgive you for preaching to them,
and it's the only way they can get a bit of their
own back."

"Kitty said I wasn't fit to have a cure of
souls."

"My dear, only a very few men *are* fit. If you
ask me, I should say that a cure of souls was the
very last thing you were cut out for."

Molly was saying what Kitty and Charlotte
had said.

"You think that of me?"

"I think that of you, and I like you all the better for it. . . . Do you know what I was really
thinking?"

"No. What?"

"Why, that you might give up your living."

"Give up my living? Give up Queningford?"

It hadn't occurred to him that this was possible.

"Yes. You can afford it now. You hate parish work. You're like me; you hate worry and responsibility. Why not go away together somewhere where there won't *be* any work or any worry, and where you won't be held responsible for the queer things other people do? There are delicious places down in Somerset and Devon."

He couldn't adjust his mind to it all at once.

"I like this house," he said, "and the garden."

Molly's voice went on, soothing, persuasive. "There are other houses and other gardens. We might find an old Elizabethan one somewhere. You know the kind of lovely, sleepy place, with clipped hedges and a walled garden and an orchard. A place you could rest in, a place where you could dream. You'd like that."

"Yes. I should like that."

And with her thick, enchanted voice her dream entered into him. A place where you could rest; a place where you could dream. Had Molly solved for him the unpleasant problem of existence?

"Nothing to do," she said, "all day long, but the things you want to do. And here you can't settle down for one minute without some stupid interruption."

"No," he said. "No. It's not an easy life."

"Give it up. Say you'll give it up. You'll never have any peace and comfort until you do."

"I'll think about it."

He thought about it half the night and all the next day. To go or stay? He loved his Rectory; he loved his church; he loved his War Memorial; he couldn't bear to leave them. And yet in his heart he knew that some day, before very long he would have left them. He would have no peace and comfort until he had given up his cure of souls.

He saw his life stretching out before him, in an unbroken succession of perfect days. Life without unpleasantness or pain. A blessed life. In a place where you could rest. A place where you could dream.